PAGE BOY

OF

CAMELOT

(Original title: Page Boy for King Arthur)

by EUGENIA STONE

Cover and illustrations by Mort Künstler

SCHOLASTIC BOOK SERVICES

NEW YORK • LONDON • RICHMOND HILL, ONTARIO

Copyright © 1949 by Eugenia Stone. This edition is published by Scholastic Book Services, a division of Scholastic Magazines, Inc., by arrangement with Follett Publishing Company.

1st printing .... November, 1967
Printed in the U.S.A.

CONTENTS

3

CHAPTER 1

*In which Tor and his
father, Wain the cowherd,
go to Camelot Castle to
ask a boon of King Arthur*

TOR raised his eyes toward the very top of the
high hill where the Castle of Camelot stood.
The hut at his back seemed to be crouching and
peering, too, out from under its thick brown thatch.
A half-grown yellow puppy lay at the boy's feet.
Tor squinted his eyes. As always, he was hoping
that a trumpet blast from the castle gate might come
down to him, faint and thin on the breeze.

5

"The wind might bring it," he said to himself, and almost made himself hear it: *Ta-rah! Ta-ta-rah!* watching to see a bold knight ride out with his squire or maybe two or three other knights. They would all look tiny at first, away up there, and then would seem to grow and brighten into blues and scarlets, until they disappeared among the oaks near the foot of the hill. In a few minutes more, there they would be, full-size, with the sun glancing on their hauberks and the wind fluttering their red and yellow pennons as they rode out of the forest.

His mother looked out over his shoulder. She was a rosy-cheeked, black-haired woman with a cheerful face. In her hands she held a brown jug half full of milk.

"Tor, it is time to take some food to the hermit. He will be hungry. Take the little loaf under your arm. Watch your step! Don't stay talking. There's much to do. But remember to ask the good man's blessing."

"Keep Fag then, Mother. He'd make me spill it."

The old hermit had been coming and going ever since Tor could remember. When he came, he lived in a small cave by the bank of the river; but where he came from or where he went at times, nobody knew or dared to inquire. The villagers knew that he had returned today, for the breeze brought the tinkle of a bell he always hung on a tree near his cave. Ratha, Tor's mother, and Wain the cowherd, his father, headman of the village, always saw to it that the hermit had fresh warm milk and good oaten bread.

A short cut through the woods brought Tor out on the riverbank. He backed carefully through a space in a hawthorn thicket and turned along the path that led to the cave.

On a seat made of branches an old man with a long white beard rested, sunning himself. He smiled when he saw Tor and waved a bony hand in greeting. Tor put down the food and knelt a moment for the hermit's blessing.

"The good Ratha's kindness is like the warmth of the sun," said the old man. "What news of the village this morning, my son? Has the wolf been killed?"

Tor sat down to wait for the jug and to give the news of the village doings.

"Bren got the wolf; he was a big one. The lambing's long over. The dun heifer calved. Father said I could call the young spotted one mine. She'll calve before long. But there isn't much news, ever, Father Kent. My father and my twelve big brothers are off to the woods and fields every day. My

7

mother and I go to the byre and milk the cows, and I drive them to pasture and look after them."

As Tor talked, the old man drank and ate the bread, his twinkling eyes on the boy. He saw a lad of twelve with good stout legs and arms and shoulders, with clear blue eyes and a mop of hair the color of sunshine. The boy had a good strong face — a little too bold for a peasant perhaps, and it might be, a bit willful. But it was a good face.

Chin on his fist, Tor looked down at the river. After a while he said:

"Father Kent, King Arthur is the greatest knight in the world, isn't he?"

The hermit nodded.

"In all Christendom there is no nobler knight."

"After him who is the greatest?"

"Next to Arthur, Sir Launcelot of the Lake is thought the noblest in all Britain. Every wicked knight fears him."

Tor's eyes glowed.

"Oh, Father Kent, if I could only be a knight and ride away on a black war horse to do great deeds!"

The hermit looked serious.

"Deeds are only great, my son, if they are good."

"I know, Father. But fighting a wicked knight to rescue a damsel in distress, or freeing a hundred prisoners from some giant's castle, would be a great deed." Tor sighed. "If there were only *some* way I could grow up to be a knight!"

Father Kent tilted the brown jug, drank the last of the milk, and set the vessel down beside him, smiling a little.

"One thing you can always do," he said.

"What is that, Father?"

"Be ready."

"Ready? Why, I'm ready now! I'd go in a minute. I'd — "

"Listen, my son. Do you know what a knight's vows are? He must be willing to right wrongs, to fight for the weak against those who oppress them and for the good against the wicked. He must be pure and loyal. He must learn obedience, for whoever commands must first know how important it is to obey. Could you promise all these?"

Tor nodded eagerly. The sun made his tumbled hair shine.

"Of course, Father, I could — all of it. It's just what I want to do."

The hermit swept up some crumbs and put them into his mouth. Tor had folded his arms, sighing a little, thinking.

The sound of a ram's horn blown vigorously came from the village. Father Kent looked questioningly at Tor, who had clasped his hands over one brown knee and was rocking himself back and forth.

"Is it true that a knight like Sir Launcelot can leap to the saddle all in armor?"

The old man nodded, his eyes twinkling under the winter-white thatching of his brows.

"That and all the other things, my son, Sir Launcelot had to learn — and to tame and ride his great black charger Beltran, the most beautiful horse in Britain."

Tor's eyes brightened.

"Beltran!" he breathed. "I've — I've seen him — I think."

"Ay," answered the hermit. "Mayhap. Many things Sir Launcelot had to learn, the first being obedience." He smiled. "And even you, my Tor, brave son of the headman of Camelot village, can learn that — or so you said."

There was something in the hermit's tone that made Tor look inquiringly into his face. Then a startled expression came into his own. He jumped to his feet.

"The horn was for me," he said hastily. "I must go."

Father Kent put up his hand in blessing and turned silently toward the cave. Tor caught up the jug and ran back along the pathway. The old hermit shook his white head, but he was still smiling as he caught the last glimpse of Tor's linen shirt and brown legs hurrying away.

At sundown one day, when Tor was just back from an afternoon in the meadows, he heard the loud sound of a trumpet from the forest. Here was excitement! With a shout he started toward the road, followed at a scamper by every boy and girl and man and woman in the village. Look! There was a slim young man riding along on a gray palfrey. From time to time the rider was putting a trumpet to his mouth to blow a blast. He waved the horn at the row of staring, grinning villagers.

"Listen, great and small, to the words of our good King Arthur: 'Being now on my way to my Castle of Camelot, with my fair bride, Queen Guinevere, I give my kingly promise to grant any boon asked by knight, squire, damsel, page, or churl.' These be the words of King Arthur of Britain."

After they had gone, and even the dust had settled, the villagers went back to their work. Tor raced for home, a wild thought whirling in his head. King Arthur had promised to grant anybody a boon. Anybody at all! Maybe his father would be willing to ask one for him! It would only be that he might have work given him to do at the castle. Ah, what a life that would be, up there among the walls and

11

towers! So excited that he could not eat his supper, he begged Wain and Ratha to give him this wonderful chance.

His father and mother listened absently for a while, but at last Ratha said to Wain:

"Husband, go with Tor and ask the boon. It will be granted, for the King gave his word."

The cowherd looked out the open door into the twilight and made no answer. Tor squirmed on his low stool, watching his father's face, not heeding the slow argument back and forth among his twelve brothers. Finally the eldest — Bren — spoke, yawning.

"Father, ask the boon for Tor. He'll keep us all from our rest. Let him go, if his heart is set on it."

Making up his mind at last, Wain spoke.

"Let be, Tor. You and I will away to the castle at the rise of sun. Now let us all sleep."

But how could Tor sleep after that? With Fag beside him, he curled down on his straw; but he felt like running from the hut out into the starlight and throwing his hands over his head, shouting and skipping along the road to cry to the night and the stars the news! He would go to the castle in the morning! His father would ask King Arthur to let him stay there — to work for his keep! He would see the knights, as close as his own brothers! He would see Sir Launcelot! He would see Beltran dance and curvet! Oh, how long it was till morning!

With the first swift arrow shot by the sun, Tor and the yawning Fag and Wain and all the rest were rousing. Remembering, Tor sprang up with a shout. Ratha, smiling into his eyes, had his clean yellow linen shirt ready.

He could scarcely eat his breakfast with talking and laughing and petting Fag, and warning him to be good. It was a sad thought to leave his dog behind, and Tor dared not even think of how lonesome he would be without his mother. But he comforted himself with the knowledge that he would see both again, and often, and by imagining the wonder he would share at the castle.

In but a short time, wearing his best cowhide sandals, Tor was walking beside Wain along the road. He looked back to wave his hand at his mother, hearing the last desperate howl of Fag, who watched with his nose to the crack of a shed door.

A throstle was trilling an early song from among the trees, and from far away in the shadowy woods came the faint "Cuck-oo" of a bird impudently telling his name.

Tor shook his long hair back on his shoulders and

whistled a reply. A little gray hare hopped from under a laurel thicket, its ears held up so that the inside showed pink, its inquisitive nose moving to catch the strange human scent of these passers-by. Wain was saying nothing, walking with long strides, *plod-plod*, in the summer dust. Tor began to keep step, his bare brown legs marking time with the red-wrapped legs of the cowherd — one-two, left-right. Once Tor stopped and stood listening.

"Father, hearken! The little dun heifer is mooing for her calf. I'll run back and take her to him. Wait for me."

Wain put out his hand.

"Bren will see to her. If you are thinking about the heifer, there is still time to turn back and grow up to become a cowherd like Bren and me. It is honest work. Or you can herd the swine, as Blaize and Solwin do, or watch the sheep." The cowherd stood looking at Tor, moving his heavy eyebrows into a puzzled frown.

Tor scuffed in the dust, saying nothing. Wain cleared his throat.

"This talk about the knights is all idleness. What has a churl to do with all that? The hermit is a good man, but he has told you overmuch. Better for you to settle to work with hayfork and sickle and milking stool."

It was the longest speech Tor had ever heard his father make. The cowherd pushed back his brown woolen cap.

"There is still time to turn back," he repeated slowly, and stood waiting, leaning on his staff. Tor glanced along to where the road wound among low-branching oaks, and then to the slant of the hill. The faint echo of a horn floated down into the woods.

"Hark! Look! Look, Father, look!"

A party of knights rode briskly toward the towers. Tor drew a quick breath.

"Let's hurry, Father!"

Wain sighed, put his staff deliberately before him, and strode on.

Nearer and nearer they came to the castle — through the woods, up the steep winding road. Tor turned now and then to wonder at sight of the brown thatches and stacks of the village so far below; then he would stare upward again at the castle walls, feeling small and smaller, but still brave, knowing Wain strode silently beside him and remembering that the King waited to grant boons. Folks were coming around the hill from the village of Camelot: men and women of all sorts and in all kinds of clothing, bright and new or faded and patched, but all going up, as Wain and Tor were, to ask a boon.

There was the drawbridge already down across the moat, with guards above watching. Wain and Tor and the others went across the bridge to enter the wide bailey, where the mighty towers of Camelot Castle reared their stone battlements toward the sky. Guided by the shouts of the King's yeomen, they trudged toward a tower where a lofty doorway stood open and a tall knight with a white wand waited.

Through the doorway the petitioners were ushered, a few at a time, while the others stood waiting. Wain looked about silently; Tor shuffled forward, little by little, dragging at his father's hand until at length they stood near the tower and it was their turn to go in.

Standing beside his father, looking into the great hall, Tor caught his breath. At the far end King Arthur, young and with light curling hair and moustache, sat on a low throne, his blue eyes keen but kind. Beside him was the beautiful Queen, with fair ladies all about her.

Never could Tor remember how he and Wain crossed the floor to kneel before these two. He could only recall that knowing he was in the very presence of King Arthur filled him with a kind of dizziness and confused awe. The tall knight with the white wand had signaled and told them what to do, and then stood back. But Tor could remember hearing his father tell in slow and simple words why they had come, and bravely ask the King's boon. The King answered kindly, and gave his order.

"Take the cowherd's son, Sir Kay," he said to the tall knight, "and give him some task about our castle. Let him abide here."

And soon Tor and his father were crossing the floor again, and going out across the bailey and to the drawbridge, Wain's big hand on Tor's shoulder.

It was hard to tell his father good-bye.

"Come home when you can, my son," said Wain. "And act as I would have you — and as your mother would wish. Good-bye."

The tall cowherd went slowly down the hill. After watching him — a strange thickness in his throat — Tor straightened his shoulders and turned back toward the towers. What should he do now?

CHAPTER 2

*In which Tor is given
work at Camelot Castle
and helps to prepare the
great hall for a feast*

A PAGE of about fourteen, a long-legged, dark-haired boy with a crow's feather in his cap, came toward Tor. He stopped and stood with his legs straddled apart, one hand on his hip, whistling through his teeth, looking the boy over. Tor waited, not knowing what to say. At last the page said:

"You, there! I'm Alin. Sir Kay the steward asked me to show you where you're to work. Come on."

He turned briskly away, looking back to add:

"Stir your shanks. I've important things to do."

Tor hurried at the heels of the page, admiring his violet-colored tunic and his cap and feather, and taking in the sights of the castle bailey as they rounded a tower and went across. It was a wide, busy yard. On every side were sheds and shops where men were working at the castle's many affairs. In the center was a well where three men were drawing water to fill jugs for several women in long, loose-sleeved tunics.

Tor sniffed. The smell of bubbling soup and roasting meat came from a cookhouse near which three small, half-clad children lingered. Past this, the nose-tickling scent of new loaves floated warm from a bake oven where two women and a short, dark man carrying a jug were stopping to look in at the bread. Passing a blacksmith's, Tor breathed the odors of burned hoofs and leather, and looked keenly at two tall black war horses and a white palfrey stamping and shaking their manes as they waited their turn.

Alin led him straight across the bailey to a flight of stone steps on the side of a tower. Up these Tor followed with as much of a skip and a jump as the page. Through a doorway they entered another stairway in the thickness of the wall. It was dim

19

here, but up skipped Alin, and up skipped Tor after him. At the top they paused together at the entrance of a high, round hall, the largest room Tor had ever seen.

He stood still a moment, blinking into the great room, where one window let in a slanting streak of sunshine. It felt almost cold in here, for the stone walls were very thick and the small window high.

Alin jerked his dark head sidewise.

"Here's your work, to help clean the floor. Gort — he's the one in the brown cap — he'll tell you what to do."

With a final superior grin, the page turned and went running down the stair. Inside the room Tor saw half a dozen barelegged men working, clad in loose linen shirts. The one who wore the brown woolen cap, catching sight of the boy at the door, called out:

"You by the door! Put those idle hands of yours to work. Help with the rushes."

The floor was thickly covered with dry rushes, yellow and brown and dusty green, tramped upon and broken by the tread of many feet. Buried among the rushes were half-gnawed bones left there by the dogs. A long table on trestles was stretched across the room; another was crosswise at its end. The first table had heavy benches beside it; at the second, there were stools and even several carved chairs such as Tor had never seen before. He stopped to gaze at the high carved backs. Some of the churls were moving the seats to scrape away the rushes under the tables.

Tor began to help, gathering up a dusty armful and following some of the other workers out into the bailey. Back and forth they went, throwing down their loads and going up for more. Tor sneezed and, while wiping his eyes on his forearm, almost fell into a square hole in the middle of the floor, where a ladder led down into a cold, dark room. But dust or no dust, he and another churl were ordered to shovel up the ashes in an immense fireplace and carry them away in baskets. Tor saw that a whole tree trunk had burned away and left the fireplace like a choked-up black cave. He tried to talk with the lean little churl he was helping. He asked the boy's name.

"Grunden," grunted the other. "What's yours? You from Camelot village?"

"Yes. I'm Tor, son of Wain the cowherd. The King said I could work here."

Another grunt was the only answer as Grunden went off with a basket of ashes.

When every big stone in the floor had been swept clean and the chimney place cleared, and while the air was still cloudy with dust, the churls began to bring in fresh green rushes and throw piles of them here and there. Tor helped to spread these under the big table and all over most of the floor, and to heap other armloads over these until they were thick and springy. Grunden came in with a small armful and threw it down.

"Here be the last of the fresh ones, Gort. What now?"

Brown-capped Gort straightened and looked, frowning.

"Fetch more. These be not enow. Sir Kay will have our hides tanned on our bodies if the seats be not well rushed today. Look after the seats where the King and Queen will sit. Then you and the new churl go get some of the finest rushes from down the moat where the bittern nests. Show him how to weave mats for the seats."

Tor and wiry little Grunden went along to the marshy spot where the best rushes were growing. After weaving some into mats, they carried them back to the tower.

These were all new and interesting things to Tor. He ran up and down the stairways, scraped, brushed, picked up old bones, and helped place the mats on the seats. As he went down with his arms full of the rushes, he noticed that churls from the other parts of the castle were adding their contributions to the big pile in the bailey. He had glimpses, too, of knights. Some of them were strolling about the bailey in bright-bordered tunics and swaying mantles; others wore closer-fitting, shorter tunics without sleeves. Some were exercising their war horses in an outer field near a long line of sheds. Two knights in full armor went clanking across the drawbridge, their squires, holding the knights' lances straight up, following behind on smaller horses. More than once Grunden had to warn Tor to keep at work, for there was no time now for dreaming.

The last of the rushes had been carried from the hall. Men and women were coming in with linen cloths and woven carpets to lay upon the tables, together with goblets, jugs, and piles of trenchers. Gort, Grunden, and the other churls left the tower room, Gort calling to Tor:

"Hearken, youngster. Burn the pile of rushes out there. Take it bit by bit, and keep watch of it."

Once more Tor hurried down the steps, thinking this part of the job would be more fun. The pile was a big one. He would have to get a bit of fire from somewhere.

A flicker from across the bailey caught Tor's searching eyes. He ran toward it, hearing the *clink-clink* of a hammer on iron. Inside was the biggest man he had ever seen, bareheaded and bare-armed, singing as he worked.

"I — I am looking for a coal," Tor stammered,

as the big man looked at him. "I have to fire the old rushes."

The smith nodded. He had a wide, soot-blackened face with thick, smiling lips showing above a coarse black beard.

"Take a coal and welcome, but bring back my tongs," he said, and went on with his hammering and singing.

Tor carried the glowing coal carefully in the grip of the tongs. Yells of laughter were coming from the tiltyard, where some of the younger squires were tilting at the quintain. This was a pole set in the ground with a shorter length of wood across the top held by a nail, so that the crosspiece would whirl. On one end of this piece was a shield, and from the other dangled a bag filled with sand. At the top of the pole a battered old helmet was set.

It took long practice and skill to strike the helmet so that the quintain did not go around; but it was fun to strike the shield, which would whirl with a doleful creak. Then, as it came around, the sandbag would catch the slow or unskillful squire with a clout that might knock him off his horse before he could gallop past.

The hackneys seemed doing their best to pretend to be war horses, just as the young squires were playing at being knights. Most of the lances missed the helmet, and several squires got a blow from the sandbag. Twice there was a fair hit on the helmet that knocked it off the pole. Then what a shout went up:

"Galahad! Galahad!"

The winner, a strong, laughing lad of about fifteen, raised his hand and waved it, reining his pretty sorrel mare around for another turn. Alin and several other pages were running about picking up dropped lances, playing at being squires themselves. Three were throwing light javelins at a target. When one of the javelins came flying into the bailey, Tor ran and got it and threw it back at the target, delighted when it made a hit and the squires shouted in surprise. Then, noticing that his coal would soon go out, he dashed across the bailey to the rush pile.

Holding the tongs with one hand and waving the coal, he kicked some of the rushes aside into a small pile and set them afire. The flames mounted quickly. Tor added another armful and another.

A shout of laughter came from the tiltyard. Taking a minute, Tor went across to see what the fun was. One of the boys was picking himself up and racing after a small brown horse. Tor watched the chase and capture. Then, remembering his fire, he went back. It was almost out. He knelt and blew on the small flame that was licking along the last broken bit of dry rush; then he fed it with small bits of leaves, greasy with dog meat, until it blazed high.

"If I make a larger fire," he was thinking, "I can go over and have more time to watch. I don't believe three armfuls would be too much. They don't take long to burn."

This seemed a good idea. He put on four armfuls and crossed again to watch the tilting.

He found that the squire who had caught the brown horse was riding him around the enclosure, now and then putting a foot back to tickle the animal in the flank. At that the horse would rear up on his hind legs suddenly, usually tumbling his rider to the ground. Everybody, including Tor, would roar with laughter. One after the other, the squires rode the brown horse, tickled his flank, and were spilled playfully by the clever brown pony.

Galahad jumped off his sorrel mare. Alin ran and caught her bridle and stood stroking her while Galahad took his turn on the brown. It was fun for everybody, including the hackney.

All at once a great hubbub came to Tor's ears from across the bailey. He jumped and looked, his heart beginning to race as he heard the shout:

"Fire! Fire!"

Black smoke and leaping flames showed above the cookhouse as he turned and ran.

CHAPTER 3

*In which Tor almost
sets fire to Camelot
Castle, and Sir Kay
sends him to work for
Kimmel the cook*

THE BLAZE had caught the big pile of rushes and flamed high, burning fast across the weed patch to the empty shop of the armorer. Already a pile of lumber stacked beside it was beginning to burn. If the shed went, the cookhouse would go, and then the mews would be in danger, to say nothing of scattered sheds and huts nearby.

Yelling churls were rushing across the bailey; even the young squires, shouting, jumped from their horses and raced to help. A fire among the wooden shops and huts in the courtyard was a dangerous thing, for they burned quickly, and drawing water from the well or moat took time. There was a beating of branches, a shrieking of orders. Gort, Grunden, and the other castle workers ran from another tower to add their cries and exertions. The churls in the cookhouse dropped their jugs and pans, and left their meat to scorch while they joined in the fight. Men, boys, and women were scraping up earth to fling on the fire, some running to the well, others to the moat. Tor, his face blistered, worked harder than he had ever worked before.

He was exhausted when the fire was conquered. He wiped his face on his arm, his heart sinking, and stared out of smarting eyes at the half-burned heap of rushes that lay scattered all about, the smoking patch where the weeds had been, and the charred side of the shed where the flames had bitten deep into the armorer's store of lumber. What had he done by his disobedience? What ought he to do now?

Once the fire was out, the excitement died away almost as quickly as it had started. The churls trotted back into the tower they were cleaning, Gort at their head. In passing, he gave Tor an angry look and shouted:

"You'll hear from Sir Kay, boy!"

The squires sauntered back to the tiltyard, Galahad with his arm over Alin's shoulder. The cooks returned to their dried-up soup and scorched meat; the knights and guards who had been watching turned within doors or strolled away. Tor, not knowing where to go, sat down beside the armorer's shed and thought painfully of what he had done. What would the steward say to him? What would Wain and Katha say when he was sent home? He dropped his smeared face into his hands and sat waiting. Soon he heard a step. It was Sir Kay. Tor stood up.

The calm steward was looking at the results of the fire, fingering his chin. Without looking at Tor, he said dryly:

"You had something to do with all this, Tor?

"Yes, Sir Kay."

"How was that?"

"I — Gort told me to burn the rushes. He told me — "

Sir Kay, holding his chin between finger and thumb considered the boy before him.

"What were you doing when it caught?"

"I — was watching the — the tilting. I stayed longer than I thought."

29

The steward pursed his lips and nodded.

"Gort," he said surprisingly, and as if more to himself than to Tor, "should have known better. But — a churl as well as a page of a squire or a knight should be obedient. What do you think?"

Tor's hands clutched the front of his shirt. He raised his eyes to Sir Kay's.

"I — I think I ought."

His eyes fell before Sir Kay's until he was looking at the ground between them. There was a long silence. Then, clearing his throat, Sir Kay said:

"There is work to be done — much work. The ashes and cinders — "

"I'll clean them up, Sir Kay!"

"Of course. After you do, you may go and tell Kimmel the cook that I sent you. Look that you are worthier of trust."

Scraping up and carrying away the ashes and charred wood was a very long, hot, and dirty job. But Tor stuck to it, his body streaming with perspiration, his hands and face and legs black with smoke and cinders. When he had taken the final basketful away and thrown it down over the hill among the clustering saplings and bushes, he went and plunged into the moat, not knowing that swimming there was forbidden. After he had cleaned himself and his shirt, he went to the cookhouse.

As he trotted across the bailey, his yellow shirt clinging and damp, he felt happier. He had done all he could to atone for his fault. Sir Kay was giving him another job; he would do better. He would never again do anything that would make more work for those people who already worked too hard. From now on he would keep his mind on his work.

As he was passing the blacksmith's shop, full of his resolves, he heard the *clink-a-clink* of the smith's hammer. Suddenly he whirled and ran back to scrabble along the edge of the burned space where he had thrown the tongs. He groaned, picked them up, and walked over to the smith's. Here again he had failed, although nobody had noticed it. Giles was too busy; the others didn't know. But Tor knew, and it was with a flushed face that he returned the tongs and thanked the smith.

The cookhouse had a hearth where large slabs of fresh meat were roasting on skewers before a pile of coals. The cook, Kimmel, was a fat, greasy man with a big, heavy nose, round popeyes, and bushy eyebrows above a red, perspiring face. Kimmel's fat body was bared to the waist, where he had tucked his loose shirt in at his belt, letting it dangle about his hips. He was going from slab to slab, turning the meat, placing a wooden platter here and there to catch the drippings, calling to a couple of churls:

"Lay on wood here. Can't you see the sun be going down? Would you have the welcoming feast tarry because of your laziness? Lay oak wood at the back there."

One of the helpers, younger than the others, answered briskly:

"I'll run for more wood, Master."

Rushing out, he jostled Tor.

"Hey! Give me room!" he shouted.

The fat cook glanced toward the doorway.

"Have you nothing to do, boy, but stare at other folk working?" he scolded, putting his hands on his fat hips.

"I have been working, Master, at the cleaning, Sir Kay sent me."

Kimmel's bushy eyebrows went up, his round eyes seemed to pop out.

"Sir Kay? Did he send you to me? Pish! I told him well and truly I wanted another man. Have you ever — do you know aught of the art of cooking, boy?"

Tor looked doubtful.

"I've watched my mother boil herbs and bake loaves. And — as for fish, and now and then a piece of venison from the woodward's share of a deer — or maybe a cony —"

The cook's mouth turned down, and he shrugged his thick shoulders. His red face was getting redder.

"A young village churl is all he sends me," he grumbled, hitching up his dangling shirt. "But I must make the best of it, woe's me! Go you and help Mob fetch wood. Be brisk!"

Mob was a shock-headed boy a few years older than Tor, very quick in his movements and way of talking. He grinned and looked at Tor out of the corners of his eyes, silently at first.

As they went back and forth with armloads of wood, they began to get acquainted and to scramble for the best pieces, to scuffle a little and giggle. Mob was friendly enough, and willing to talk when ever Kimmel gave them a chance.

The fire flamed up and died back over the coals. The roasting meat must be watched and turned, and not allowed to scorch again. In the midst of all the work, a freckle-faced youth came across from the mews to ask for the cooked meat for the falcons. Tor was sent with him.

There was much going to and from the oven in the courtyard by Kimmel and a big-eared churl with a wooden tray. As the time for the feast approached, there was more and more rushing about. Tor got into everybody's way, trying to help, and dodged a clout on the ear from Kimmel.

"Go help fill the beakers," he shouted. "Mob,

take this varlet and get the morat ready for drinking. Fill up the beakers and the leathern bottles yonder. Grizzal, do you whittle more skewers and have them ready."

In the shed behind the cookhouse Tor and Mob, working together, soon had bottles and beakers filled with the sweet-bitter honey drink. As they worked, they heard from across the bailey the blare of a horn.

"There blows the washing horn," said Mob. "The knights and damsels will soon be gathering for the feast. Dip another beaker of the morat, Tor. The King likes it well, so Kimmel says."

"Make fast your shirt, Grizzal. Go wash the sweat off your face, Mob. Put on your sandals, Brad. Knot that thong, you there. Now Ald, you and Brad take up the meat and carry the trenchers shoulder-high. Mind your manners. Hold the meat to each guest so he may cut off what he likes. Dunnal, go behind with another beaker, and you, Hammeth, see that you don't spill the morat in filling the goblets. Go once around the table and return for more. Hold up your heads and step lightly, like this. Don't kick up the rushes nor stumble over the dogs. Tor, carry the two leathern bottles of morat," ordered the cook.

The procession, headed by the fat Kimmel himself carrying a wand, marched out of the cookhouse

— trenchers and trays held shoulder-high, bottles and beakers full — and took its way, Tor last of all, across to the towers. Struggling with the two heavy bottles of morat, Tor toiled up the stairs and stood, as Kimmel had bidden him, just outside the door of the feasting hall.

There were cheerful sounds of laughter and talk from inside, and then the music of a harp and the sound of a voice singing. A shout of laughter went up as the nasal voice of the jester cut through the sudden yelp of a hound. Tor put down his leathern bottles and looked around.

It was the same hall where he had worked so hard with the rushes. But now the big room was gay with knights and ladies at the cloth-spread tables. He could see Sir Launcelot with his son Galahad standing behind him. Kimmel was marching around the tables, leading his servingmen toward where King Arthur and Queen Guinevere sat. Torches were flaring here and there, some on the wall, others held by pages near the tables. Alin was holding one near Galahad and Sir Launcelot. Now Mob was offering Sir Launcelot meat, and the knight was cutting off a piece. Kimmel himself was filling a goblet for the King.

Back came Grizzal for another bottle — and Brad for the second, and with a message from Kimmel to hurry back and mend the fire and the skewer more meat. Tor ran back, his mind full of what he had seen.

"King Arthur's chair was the one with the carved dragon's head on the back and the dragon's claws for feet," he thought, skewering a slab of meat, "and the fair Queen's the one with the eagle's head and the curved wings. The King's hound, Cavall, was lying close to him — just the way Fag lies close to me. Galahad looked tall in that silver-colored tunic. He took the leathern bottle from Hammeth and filled Sir Launcelot's goblet while Alin held the torch steady."

Here came the servingmen hurrying down the stairway for more food and drink, with Kimmel following, puffing, calling for another beaker of morat.

"Stand ready there — the meat — the fresh loaves! Tor, stay and watch the oven. Forward again!"

When the feasting was over, the churls and Kimmel ate. Tor was nearly famished, for he had had but little to eat since he left home. The remains of the feast offered more varieties of food than he was accustomed to, and he ate greedily. Afterward the cook and his helpers went wearily to their beds of straw in the small wooden huts near the cookhouse.

Tor lay down near Mob, thinking of Galahad standing behind Sir Launcelot, and of Alin holding the torch close to Galahad's shoulder. It was wonderful to work at the castle. Mob began to snore. Then Hammeth began to wheeze, and Grizzal to make little buzzing noises. Ald grunted and made a whistling sound through his lips. Tor listened. All around him they were asleep and snoring, the way his brothers snored — yes, and the way Fag sometimes snored too. Only Fag would give a little yelp now and then and thump his tail. Tor sighed. He wondered if his mother was asleep. She never snored. Bren didn't either. Wain had a big, hearty, snorting kind of snore. As Tor thought of home, a great wave of loneliness swept over him. All these folk who lay about him were strangers. He wished he could feel the comfort of Fag's rough, warm body cuddled up against him. And what would he not give to snuggle up against Ratha and feel her arms about him, caressing him even in her sleep!

Tor's lip quivered and his eyes felt wet. He was ashamed to feel like crying, a great boy of twelve here at the wonderful castle where he had longed to be. But he was weary and homesick, and he thought perhaps it would be better to stay home after all. Tomorrow he would go home, to his mother's loving arms and his father's gentle strength, and his big brothers and Spotty — and Fag. Comforted by the thought, Tor fell asleep.

CHAPTER 4

*In which Tor and Bolar
ride Agricola to the hunt
and see old Sowker, the
fierce wild boar*

AS ALWAYS, with morning the world looked
brighter. Tor had forgotten the fears and
loneliness of the night before, and decided to stay
on at the castle for a while longer at least. Soon perhaps he would find a chance to run home and tell
Ratha about the exciting things he had seen. But
as the days went by, Tor had little time for himself. He began to be become acquainted with the

ways of the churls who labored at the castle for the great folk who lived within it. He helped the women draw water, and soon knew their children and was friends with them and their dogs. There were many dogs owned by the knights and the King, but not very many loose in the bailey. Tor was thankful Fag had been left at home to learn the care of sheep from Blaize. Fag would surely have been in trouble most of the time with the often quarrelsome mongrels belonging to the churls.

Following the sounds of yelps and barking, Tor had found the way to the kennels very soon. These sheds, with a sleeping room above for the kennel boys, were built over near a postern gate leading out into a meadow. The dog boys, busy with cleaning and combing the animals, had little time to give to visiting. But Bolar, a grimy, snub-nosed boy of about Tor's age, wearing only a rag of a shirt tied about him with a leather strap, was ready to tell Tor everything he himself knew.

"The big black and white ones — *e*-normous, ain't they? — they be called alaunts. They can make the ground fly under 'em, they can. The ones with the broad chests and good legs be half mastiff and half hound. They're limmers, and they're fierce! They hunt the wild boar. The slim ones are gazehounds. Look at the bright eyes of them and the way they hold their heads up." Bolar pointed proudly. "They see the game first and give tongue. The brachells across there by the shed, they can't see so far, but they can track anything by scent. Aye, these be wonderful dogs, Tor!"

It was fascinating to linger around the kennels, listening to Bolar's dog lore; to hear stories of stag hunts and boar hunts. Tor heard tales of old Sowker, the fierce wild boar that had evaded hunters and hounds alike for many a season. Though he had been sighted again and again, and even brought to bay by the dogs, the wily, savage beast always escaped without harm. But often the hunters and the dogs bore the marks of his vicious tusks.

Sometimes Tor helped with the grooming of the dogs, and sometimes he went with the entire pack and all the boys into the meadows for a frolic. Tor learned to know every dog. But the one he was really fondest of belonged solely to Bolar. He was a bowlegged, broad-headed, heavy-jawed yellow mongrel that Bolar said wasn't any special kind of dog, but was just plain dog. His name was Hodge.

"See them jaws?" Bolar asked, rolling and tumbling with the dog in the grass. "When Hodge takes hold of anything with them jaws, he just *never* lets go! He's a wonder, he is!"

It was fun to know Bolar. Besides owning Hodge, the boy possessed an old chestnut horse called

40

Agricola which a knight had given to Bolar's own grandfather. The animal was actually a charger! Tor's pride was almost too much to bear when Bolar took him up behind for a stiff gallop around the meadow on old Agricola. Of course, it wasn't a comfortable gallop. Agricola's hips were like battlements, and his back like the roof of a house that badly needed thatching. But there was still plenty of life in the old horse, as anybody could tell by the glint in his one good eye, the gay whisk of his nearly bald tail, and the gallant cock of his pointed ears.

Another of Tor's new friends was the big, hearty smith, Giles, who proved to be as full of tales of battles with giants and false and wicked knights as was Father Kent. Then, too, the smith could tell marvelous stories of the magic of the old wizard named Merlin who lived, off and on, in one of the highest towers, where he could watch the stars. King Arthur himself, so Giles said, was always guided by the wisdom of the old magician, who really knew everything.

But of all his new friends, Tor liked Brok the armorer best. Brok was a small man, stoop-shouldered and with a dark purple scar down one lean cheek. His eyes were always kind. He talked about horses, too, and weapons.

Brok showed Tor lances he was making for Sir

41

Gawaine and Sir Caradoc. The armorer was also making a new hauberk for King Arthur. Tor watched whenever he could take the time. Brok showed him how he punched and laced the leather foundation and then, very carefully, one by one and row by row, fastened overlapping, small gilt plates so that neither arrow, sword, nor spear could pierce between. Merlin, so Brok said, had warned the King to have a new hauberk made, for the stars foretold that before long there would be hard fighting with the fierce blond Saxons.

Sometimes Tor wandered across to the large stables where the war steeds stamped and whinnied. The churls and the squires were always working among them. Warned to keep out of the way, Tor would go as near as he dared, especially to the big shining Beltran, the charger of Sir Launcelot. Once as he was going toward these stables, Tor saw Sir Launcelot ride across the bailey on Beltran, his helmet hanging at his knee, his sword about his neck by a broad strap, his lance in rest, his shield hanging over his shoulder. Tor stopped and stared at the wonderful sight of the most famous knight of the Round Table riding away on his black charger. Gorman, Sir Launcelot's squire, who was standing watching longingly, answered Tor's unspoken question.

"He goes on a mission — and he would go alone."

Gorman sighed and turned away, and Tor ran over to the tiltyard, where the young squires were tilting at an iron ring hung by a thread. He was just in time to see Galahad, racing his sorrel mare Lila across the yard, put his lance through the ring and carry it off at a gallop.

One morning Bolar came running wildly across the bailey with news that the woodward had reported that old Sowker, the wild boar that had so long been doing mischief, had been sighted and trailed to a lair somewhere along the river. There was to be a boar hunt at once.

Tor and Bolar ran back to the kennels, where all was excitement. Knights in padded tunics were gathering, mounted on their hunting horses. The brachells and the limmers were to be taken. The three largest dog boys were to go to look after them, and ride double with some of the yeomen if the pace became too fast.

Across the bailey rode the knights at a trot, Sir Gawaine leading, his silver hunting horn slung over his shoulder. Each knight carried a boar spear. The brachells and limmers were yelping after the horses, held in leash by the shouting, straining dog boys. At the drawbridge King Arthur, in green cap and tunic, joined them. Tor and Bolar, running after, watched the hunt ride off, clattering across the bridge and away.

"Let's follow!" suggested Tor. "We can run. Kimmel won't want me until — We could get back — "

"We couldn't keep up!" Bolar shook his tousled head disconsolately. "They'll go fast. The woodward said old Sowker has a den in a pile of rocks up river. We'd never be able to make it."

They turned back, walking with their heads down. Tor felt as if he could hardly stand it to go through the day, all the while knowing that the hunt — and King Arthur — were away galloping through field and glade and over hill and vale. Galahad was with them, and even Alin had gone. The two were riding shoulder to shoulder, their horses dancing with excitement. Oh, what wouldn't it be like if he could go!

Suddenly Bolar was gripping his arm, shouting.

"Agricola! Agricola! We'll ride old Agricola! Come on!"

Without another word they ran. It took almost no time at all to reach the ancient charger, dozing in the shade of a tree. He raised his head slowly and looked kindly at them with his one good eye. There were the thong bridle and the ragged fold of blanket where Bolar had dropped them. Swiftly they bridled Agricola and clambered somehow to his high, bony back. Catching the excitement, and full of clover and sudden ambition, he took them at a stiff and rickety gallop across the bailey, where early toilers stopped to gape in amazement, across the bridge and down the hill. Yelping and cavorting behind them followed Hodge, every tooth showing, his tongue flopping and his tail in the air.

The boys knew where to go. There were old Druid rock piles among the oaks far up the stream. It was there the woodward had said old Sowker had his hide-out. They crossed by the ford and headed up the farther side.

For some time they were too far behind even to hear the faintest sounds of the chase. Then they thought they caught the sounding of the horn.

"They've — they've sighted him! Hold on tight, Tor!"

Gallant Agricola was doing his best, breathing hard and pounding along the soft turf. They entered the woods at the side of a hill and came upon the horses of the hunters, with men left to take care of them. The hunters and dogs had gone forward to harry old Sowker out of his lair in the rocks. Tor and Bolar scrambled off Agricola and ran forward, leaving the old horse standing near the others.

Deep thickets were growing among scattered

rocks. The boys broke through. In an open space beyond, just below a rocky hillside, the hunters were crouching in a half circle, each man holding his boar spear with the end to the ground and the point slanting toward the entrance to old Sowker's den. The brachells were barking behind the circle; the limmers, in a crazy, yelping pack, were charging at bushes.

There was a savage grunting and squealing. In a rush, a ferocious black animal with hot, little red eyes, vicious tusks curving up from his jaws, and a bristle of mane like a stiff ruff from his head to his shoulders, dashed out of the thicket, his little knot of a tail almost straight with fury.

The limmers rushed him. One reached his ear, but was shaken off yelping with pain; another flew into the air, howling from the blow of the heavy head, the upsweep of the tusks. The other limmers hung back, watching for a better chance, yelping wildly, mad to get at the boar.

Old Sowker faced them, his black jowls dripping, his small eyes gleaming like coals of fire, his gory tusks ready to meet any dog brave or rash enough to attack him. There was a sudden shriller yelp and what looked like a streak of yellow fur flying through the thicket. Something had come up behind Sowker and seized him by the tail.

"It's Hodge!" yelled Bolar, pounding Tor on the back. "It's Hodge! Get him! Get him, Hodge!"

Hodge needed no encouragement. What he seized, he held. Old Sowker whirled and grunted and squealed with fury. He tried to slash and missed. The limmers, seeing their chance, dashed in again to the attack. Hodge was swinging back and forth, his jaws clamped until, with the severed end of the tail in his mouth, he fell in one direction while Sowker, in a frenzy of rage, dashed through the yapping limmers in another.

With a shout, Sir Gawaine set his spear. The boar swerved, clearing the point by a hair. Every hunter was hot after him now, together with the brachells and the baying limmers and Hodge, silent because of the end of the tail still firmly held in his teeth.

King Arthur, who was nearest to the boar, flung his spear. It pierced Sowker's back, but not deep enough to wound him badly. Stung and furious, the creature turned and charged straight at the King, losing the spear as he came.

Arthur faced the boar stanchly, drawing his dagger, but it was a poor defense against the raging beast. In a second, Tor thought to see the King slashed by the maddened boar's bloody tusks.

A shower of spears flashed through the air, but, hastily thrown, most of them missed their mark.

Those that struck, the furious Sowker shook off, hardly interrupted in his charge to destroy this isolated enemy.

Then a strong young body ran before Arthur, hurling a short spear that found the boar's heart. It was Galahad risking his life for his King. As old Sowker reared and fell, spume from his snarling jaws spattered both Galahad and Arthur.

A shout of joy and relief went up — from hill and stones and woods to the very sky. "Arthur! Galahad!"

It was a happy, thankful party that rode away from the old Druid stones, along the quiet river, and up the hill to the castle. Far behind the knights marched a group of sturdy yeomen carrying old Sowker on their spears. Still further behind, going at a very low walk, plodded Agricola. His tail switched now and then, his ears were still up, his one eye determined as ever, but his old legs were all tired out. Tor and Bolar walked happily just ahead of him, talking, boasting to each other of Hodge, of Agricola, and of themselves. It had been a glorious hunt.

Hodge, one ear up and one ear down, was investigating trees and bushes along the way as if nothing of importance had happened. He had carefully buried the end of Sowker's tail near the root of a tree.

That night, in the huge hall, there was a great feasting on fresh pork. The boar's head, cleaned and cooked, wreathed with crisp leaves and with an apple in its mouth, was carried proudly to the table by Kimmel himself.

After the feast King Arthur, laughing, sent the cook out to the kennels with a choice bone for Hodge.

Kimmel was so pleased at the notice King Arthur and Queen Guinevere had taken of him, and the applause he had received when he carried in the boar's head, that he no more than cuffed Tor and sent him sprawling for going to the hunt.

CHAPTER 5

*In which Tor visits
his family and tells them
wonderful tales, and
makes a new friend*

TOR had been at the castle for two weeks before
he had a chance to go home. One day Kimmel
sent the boy on a search for herbs that took him
near the village, and he hurried to the thatched
hut of Ratha and Wain. Kimmel had given him
leave to stay the night.

Such a joyful yelping as Fag set up when he saw
Tor! Such a smothering of hugs as Ratha embraced
him!

50

"Good Fag, I thought you'd have forgotten me," Tor cried, throwing a stick for the dog to run after. "Oh, Mother, wait till you hear the stories I have to tell! So many things have happened I'll never be able to tell about them all in one night."

Ratha looked at her son fondly. "And now, may-hap, a jug of milk and a bit of the loaf will taste good. Soon your father and brothers will be home from the fields, and all can hear your tales."

But there were tales for Ratha alone, as she busied herself about the fire. Tor found himself talking about the lonely nights when he missed them all so much, and Ratha especially.

"Aye, Tor, I can't believe you wouldn't be lonesome away off at the castle, no matter how many great folk you saw. But you'll be wanting to go back?"

"Oh yes! It's wonderful there, Mother, truly it is! And if I work hard and do my duty, I may get tasks that be more to my liking. I don't think I would ever be much at cooking, though I try my best."

"You must have known, my son," Ratha said, smiling, "that if a knight is to be strong enough to ride away and do battle, someone must see to it that he has meat. Even knights and kings must eat, and mayhap even more than most."

Wain and Blaize came home, with Bren and Solwin and the others straggling in after them. The evening meal over, they sat around listening to Tor's excited accounts of life at the castle.

He told about the first day, and how he helped to clean the hall for the feasting: ". . . King Arthur sat in a dragon chair . . . and the Queen in a chair with an eagle's head and curved arms. She looked beautiful; and Mother, she is kind, and even smiled at me! And the King is brave and tall; and Sir Launcelot, what a sight it is to see him ride off on Beltran! He is gone off on a mission now — all alone, too. He would not take Gorman, his squire, and no one knows where Sir Launcelot is."

The fire died down as Tor talked and talked. ". . . and I have a friend called Bolar. He has a dog, Hodge — and even a horse, old Agricola." Here Tor launched into a description of the boar hunt that made his listeners' eyes fairly pop from their heads.

"Finally it was Galahad who was bravest of all," he ended. "Everyone cheered him and King Arthur, and maybe Galahad a little more than the King even."

"Truly, these be great tales," Wain said, his mouth opening in a vast yawn. "But bodies be weary after a day in the fields, and dawn comes all too soon, eh Blaize? We must to bed."

Tor slumbered happily, nestled against his mother, with Fag curled up on the other side.

The sun was peeping over the rim of the world when Ratha stirred in the morning and busied herself with preparing food. One by one the others got up, until at last only Tor lay sleeping. Ratha shook him gently.

"Up, Tor, up! Your master will be looking for you at the castle."

Tor roused himself, rubbing his eyes. When he saw his mother and the others, it seemed almost as if his life at the castle was but a dream from which he had wakened. Out in the byre, Spotty mooed for her newborn calf, and his father and brothers plodded about at the morning tasks.

"You'll need to hurry, Tor," said his mother, and then Tor realized that it was no dream, and Kimmel would indeed be watching for him. Some of the herbs he would need for the soup that very day.

Quickly he ate the food Ratha had prepared — bread and milk and juicy ripe blueberries. His mother gave him a bit of bread and cheese to take with him, and Tor said good-bye to his family.

"Come back as soon as you can, my son," Ratha said, looking after him fondly.

"Aye," said the sober Wain. "See to it, lad, that you do well the tasks that are given you. No one has room for a poor and thoughtless worker."

Tor ran along the path until he was out of breath; then he stopped in the woods to gather the herbs Kimmel wanted. Birds caroled in the trees, and Tor stopped to look at them. He chased hares and small beasts among the bushes, and sought out one thing after another. The sun was high in the sky before he crossed the moat and entered the bailey.

Fat Kimmel saw him coming, and stood waiting, hands on hips.

"I could have grown the herbs and had time to spare," he grumbled. "Take them to Mob and help him with the washing. Then give them to Grizzal, for he needs them to flavor the soup."

Kimmel went off grumbling, and Tor hurried to do his bidding. He *was* late, he thought. But the morning was so fair, and the berries so sweet and juicy. . . .

Tor worked hard the rest of the day to atone for his tardiness. He was weary as he lay down to sleep that night.

Only the youngest squires had their horses on Tor's side of the castle. Galahad's beautiful young mare, Lila, was in a small shed of her own. She was the finest of all the hackneys, a slim, graceful sorrel, and she could dash across the meadow with the swiftness of a swallow. Tor loved to look at her, and to watch Galahad and Alin brush and pet her. He could see that both loved her.

Once, gathering a handful of the tenderest clover, Tor stole softly into the little shed when the mare was standing alone. She turned to eye him watchfully for a minute, stamping one forefoot impatiently, putting her nose against him inquiringly as she took the clover.

"Lila!" he whispered. "Lila!"

His hand traveled down her neck, feeling the satin of her coat and its warmth, and then down a slender foreleg. She blew through her nostrils, her nose against his back.

"Good girl."

He stood up slowly, and she was willing to let him run his hand down her nose; then she nibbled his fingers a little with her lips. Tor loved the feeling.

"She — she likes me!" he thought. "She's my friend!"

Tor picked up a brush and brushed her all over until her coat looked like shining copper, talking gently to her all the while. He was so busy and so happy that he did not know how long he had been with her. As he was combing her tail, Galahad, followed by Alin, came into the shed.

Alin whistled.

"What are *you* doing here?" he asked. "Galahad, see who's here! Who told you —"

Galahad put his hand on Alin's shoulder. Tor was standing, brush in hand, his face red.

"I — I didn't think you'd care, " he said to Galahad. "She's so — pretty. I just thought I'd brush her a bit."

He stopped and put down the brush.

Alin hooted.

"He just thought, Galahad! A churl *thought!* What do you think about that?"

But Galahad wasn't paying any attention to Alin. He was looking at Lila, who had turned her large eyes toward him.

"Lila," he said, "did you like it, girl? Did you like Tor's brushing? Tell me."

The mare nuzzled his hand and blew into his palm. Galahad laughed.

"You did a good piece of work on her mane, Tor," he said. "And her coat is beautiful. Just put the rope on her neck and lead her out to water, will you? Then turn her into the pasture."

After that, there was scarcely a day when Tor didn't find a few minutes to visit with Lila when he thought she would be alone. He felt that she really expected him, and it almost seemed that she did.

She would swing her head around toward him and stamp; and one day, when he stopped at the door a minute, Lila nickered softly. Tor went and put his arms around her neck. "You like to have me come, don't you?" he said softly.

The only thing that was unpleasant about his visits to Lila was the chance that Alin might find him there. Every time the page came upon Tor with Lila, he jeered at him.

"What does a kitchen churl know about horses?" Alin would ask. "If you came without clover, Lila wouldn't even look at you."

Tor was annoyed at Alin's teasing and sarcasm, but he did not pay too much heed to what Alin said, since Galahad himself had allowed him to talk to Lila and pet her and feed her. How Tor loved those times with the beautiful mare!

But these times were short. There were many things to be done at the cookhouse, and Tor, trying to keep his mind on his job, would tell Lila good-bye and go back to greasy and bustling old Kimmel.

It was a happy day for Tor when Sir Kay, sending for him, told him that Kimmel didn't need him any longer. What the fat cook had said to Sir Kay was:

"A cook, Sir Kay, I can never make of that boy. He spills the fat in the fire, lets the meat scorch or the fire die too low. He must be going off to watch the tilting, or to work about young Galahad's mare and come back smelling of the stable, so that he cannot be sent into the hall." Kimmel shrugged his thick shoulders. "He must even run off to follow the hunt! Give me Grundel to help me, if it please you, Sir Kay. I might make a cook of him!"

The grave and kindly steward told Tor none of this, but only said:

"Go to Argon, the falconer, at the mews. He needs someone to help besides Rimbot. Tell him I sent you."

Tor went off gladly enough. He was thankful to be quit of Kimmel's greasy pots and hot kitchen. But in the back of his mind was an uneasy feeling that again he had failed to please. He thought of the many occasions on which he had forgotten to do an errand in the excitement of some new discovery about the castle; of Mob come running for him just in time to save him from Kimmel's heavy hand; of the times when there had been no one to save him, and he had received the punishment he felt he deserved.

But no amount of slaps seemed sufficient to make Tor remember the burning meat when Galahad rode by on Lila, or when the Queen and her ladies, mounted on palfries and attended by knights and squires, crossed the moat and galloped away. In his mind Tor went with them, and he dreamed on until the cook's greasy hand jerked him back to reality.

But all that was behind him, Tor resolved. Here was a new chance, and he was determined to keep his mind on his work and to deserve praise, not punishment, from Argon — and from Sir Kay as well.

CHAPTER 6

*In which Tor becomes
helper to Argon, the chief
falconer, and goes to
the hawking*

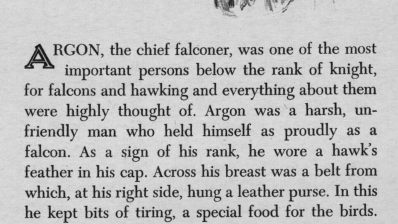

ARGON, the chief falconer, was one of the most important persons below the rank of knight, for falcons and hawking and everything about them were highly thought of. Argon was a harsh, unfriendly man who held himself as proudly as a falcon. As a sign of his rank, he wore a hawk's feather in his cap. Across his breast was a belt from which, at his right side, hung a leather purse. In this he kept bits of tiring, a special food for the birds.

His tunic of green had a narrow yellow border embroidered with red. On his feet he wore sandals as light as Sir Kay's.

The chief falconer looked at Tor doubtfully.

"Hm! There is so much to learn that you will not be able to hold it in that yellow head of yours until you are a man. If you will obey the rules of falconry and my orders, I will try to make a falconer of you. Now go you into the hackhouse and clean the perches of the young eyases. Mind you don't jerk about or sing or call out. The first thing to learn is never to startle the birds. Rimbol is there. He will show you."

Tor tiptoed past the big white gerfalcon sitting with closed eyes on her stump. He knew that this was the best loved of all King Arthur's falcons.

"The King is going to give her to the Queen," Brok had said. "She's the finest falcon in Britain, a very queen of a bird."

The darkened inner shed was full of perches. At one side several eyases, or young hawks, were sitting, their heads drawn down toward their shoulders. A group of merlins stood, each on a single leg, across from the eyases. A larger falcon rested silently in a corner, and a row of goshawks sat along a smaller, higher perch at one end of the mews.

The Falconer's helper, a freckle-faced, heavy-eyed boy of about sixteen, seemed glad to see Tor.

"It's been lonely here," he said. "Maybe you and I can talk together sometimes, when we're not in the mews — but we've got to be quiet in here or Master will be angry." But as they worked, he told Tor a few things in a whisper.

"These be branchers, old enough to hop from nest to branch. These two be lentners, caught at the time of Lent. The one in the corner is a haggard."

Tor liked Rimbot. The two worked quietly, cleaning the floor and the woven screens that hung below the perches. Then Rimbot brought out some little tubs to be washed and refilled, dropping several with a clatter, stooping hastily to pick them up, and dropping more — looking scared at the noise he had made.

"Do they drink from these?" asked Tor, as he helped pile the tubs outside.

Rimbot shook his head.

"Not they. You'd not be like to see one drink in a year. They bathe in the little tubs. Be careful not to fill them to the brim. The master won't like it if they overflow."

There was a great deal to remember. It was good hard training for a boy used to forgetting. Rimbot showed Tor many things. He was a gentle, bungling sort of a boy, very kind and careful with the birds, but apt to spill things, or break something, or forget what he was told — at which times Argon would cuff him. Once he showed Tor his back, where the marks of blows still showed.

"Master's trying to make me a good falconer," he explained. "But sometimes I wish I could live down in the village and be a shepherd or a swineherd. I could have friends down there. But maybe you and I — "

"We can be friends," said Tor, "if you like."

Sometimes Argon sent them down into the valley to catch eels for the birds. At these times Tor took Rimbot to the village to see Ratha and Fag, Wain, and as many of his brothers as were at home. Tor thought it wonderful to have more chances to go home. Rimbot thought it wonderful too, and all of Tor's family liked the clumsy, blundering boy and were somehow sorry for him.

"This be odd," Wain said. "Here be a boy who would be a shepherd and needs must be a castle helper!"

Whenever Tor had time, he went to see Lila. If Galahad and Alin were there, he would linger outside, watching for them to bring her out. Galahad would hail Tor with a raised hand and a word of greeting as they passed, but Alin would brush by, paying him no attention. Tor always knew that Lila looked at him swiftly and tossed her head.

One afternoon Alin came riding Lila back. Galahad had been called to the castle. He turned her into the grass and Tor stopped to speak to the mare.

"The Queen and some of her damsels and knights are going hawking tormorrow morning," Alin remarked, yawning. "King Arthur has gone to Caerleon."

Tor's eyes widened. Here was excitement!

"Are you going?"

Alin pulled a bunch of grass and then flung it down, frowning.

"I'd give anything to go. But I'm being sent with a message down to Camelot village. Galahad's going to ride Lila and attend the Queen."

Tor thought of the hawking all the rest of the day. At night he was tired from a trip to the valley, and from the usual cleaning and a special run with Rimbot to fly a long-winged, blue-legged lanner. Besides, he had been running about the bailey sheds and storehouses to find a mouse. Argon wanted it to mix with stewed eels for a sick hawk's supper. Despite all his weariness, the excitement of thinking about tomorrow kept Tor awake. Argon had said that he could go. This time there would be fun, and no disobedience to regret afterward. What a day he would have!

It was very early when Argon sent Tor and the

sleepy, stumbling Rimbot off with well-trained goshawks on their wrists. These birds were for use in case a cony or a hare should be started. Sunshine was coming across the bailey in a long slant, leaving a stretch of shadow reaching out from the foot of every tall tower and low workshed. The falconer had stayed in the mews a few minutes to adjust the lunys of the white gerfalcon, which Queen Guinevere herself was to fly at a pheasant.

"Go down with speed. But carry the goshawks steadily. Wait for me near the ford," Argon directed, refastening the bell on the bird's leg. "We must have them well quieted before the party comes along. I'll join you soon."

The two boys started across the bailey, holding the little goshawks on leather wrist guards, trying not to shake them. Tor's heart was light. He began to whistle shrilly, but thought of the goshawk, which must be kept quiet, and stopped. As they were passing near the silent tiltyard, Tor saw Alin running from one of the towers, his dark hair flying.

"Tor!" the page called, when he saw the two with the goshawks hurrying along. "Come help me with Lila. Galahad has to wait on the Queen. He asked me to get Lila all ready before Gorman and I leave for Camelot. Hurry, will you?"

Tor hesitated. But it wouldn't take long just to

do that, and he didn't like to refuse Alin. Besides, he suddenly remembered, catching his breath, that he had taken the buckles off the bridle straps yesterday afternoon to polish them and, hearing Rimbot calling, had laid them down and run across to the hut behind the mews for supper. He had meant to return, but — well, he had just forgotten.

"They'll be in the pile there in the corner," he thought, "and I can sort them out and put the thing together in a minute."

Rimbot hadn't stopped. He was already letting himself out at the postern gate. Alin was going with his quick stride toward Lila's shed, whistling between his teeth.

"I'll hurry; I'll be able to overtake Rimbot," Tor said to himself, turning back toward the tiltyard.

Inside the shed, Lila pricked up her small ears and looked around, whinnying softly. She wanted a bit of breakfast — clover would do — and she longed for a morning gallop. Here were two of her best friends to supply her with both. Tor hunted for something to put the goshawk on. Then he ran out into the meadow and pulled clover enough to fill the front of his tunic. Lila could be eating it while he put the bridle together.

Alin was fussing with the saddlecloth, shaking it and smoothing it on Lila's sleek back. Tor gave the clover to her with a pat on the neck and went over to the corner, where he found the straps and buckles as he had left them.

Alin put up the saddle, drawing the girth under the mare, fastening the straps, letting fall the stirrup. His motions were sure and swift. Tor tried to be as quick, thinking anxiously of Rimbot down the trail, glancing now and then at the goshawk, sitting on a stick, motionless. The bird was taking no harm, and he could surely run smoothly — holding out his arm — and catch up with Rimbot. She'd not turn a feather.

There! The straps assembled and buckled, Tor lifted the headstall and put it over Lila's head gently, taking care that each soft ear was pointed up through, stopping a moment to whisper her name and pat her nose.

"All done," he announced, passing Alin, taking up the goshawk, and running out. As he crossed the tiltyard at a smooth trot, he saw Calahad run to the shed where Alin was leading out the dancing Lila. Tor stopped to watch the lithe young squire spring into the saddle and gallop away. He heard the quick tattoo of her hoofs across the drawbridge. The rest of the party must have gone already! It was a disturbing thought. Tor hurried toward the postern.

Neither the falconer nor Rimbot was in sight. But Rimbot could be, of course, down among the trees on the hillside. Tor hastened down. The woods trail ahead was empty as far as he could see.

"Maybe he's already at the ford. Oh, I didn't know I was taking so long!"

Leaving the path, Tor cut through the trees. Here were smaller, closer-growing saplings that seemed scrambling up the hill in an eager green company, with bushes climbing among them. In as straight a descent as he could follow, Tor went down, scrambling, sliding, but not without disturbing the goshawk. She roused and fluttered her wings. Losing more time as he stopped to quiet her, Tor finally reached the bottom of the hill and went toward the ford. When he got there, thrusting through a drooping clump of willows that were leaning to look at themselves in a pool, Tor stood staring. A lump constricted his throat.

Away up the side of the stream the hawking party was sweeping at a gallop, the early sunshine bright on gay mantles of knights and squires and the fluttering scarves of damsels. Tor could hear the laughter and song, but it came more and more faintly as the brilliant cavalcade, cantering freely, turned away from the riverside into the broad, grassy land beyond. Argon and Rimbot, sturdy and long trained for this, were running steadily after the horses.

It was a beautiful morning. A dome of soft blue rose far above river and meadow, and just enough morning breeze whispered by to stir the damp hair from Tor's forehead and to bring him the scent of wild lilacs from the hills. But all this meant nothing to him now. After only a moment's horrified glance, he began to run, holding his arm as steady as he could. The ruffled goshawk swayed, moving her talons to a firmer grip, and lowered her feathers uneasily. She was disturbed and angry at Tor's unsteady gait.

A long way up the river, a spread of water made a marsh where rushes and blue water hyacinths grew. A black-crowned bittern rose in a quick spiral until it was out of sight. The party was turning to gallop along the edge of the marsh where the grasses grew tall and bushes thick. There were pheasant runs among the bushes, and it was here that the falconer hoped to flush one of the handsome birds. Running and panting, Tor still managed to keep his eyes on the thicket, watching for the startled upward flight of a fugitive. Sure enough, he made out, in a minute, the sudden swift rising of a long-tailed bird. Then he could see that the

Queen had taken and let fly the white gerfalcon.

The big bird opened her broad snowy wings to soar upward in ever-widening circles, her feathers glinting silver in the sun. No match for the falcon on the wing, the fleeing pheasant sought desperately for cover.

Underneath the flying birds the fowlers swept shouting across the meadow, spurring their mounts, all eyes watching the drama in the sky.

Away raced the white palfrey of Queen Guinevere, whose veil streamed behind like a crimson pennon. Hard after pounded knight and lady, page and squire, shouting with excitement. Tor could see Galahad riding close to the Queen, his wide shoulders straight, his lithe body swaying with Lila's easy gallop.

Argon and Rimbot, now left behind, were running, hoping to catch up with the chase at the striking of the pheasant.

From the marsh wild ducks were rising, to fan out in scared flight away down the river toward the safety of their rush-bordered lake. Far above its laboring prey, the falcon wheeled.

"She stoops! She stoops!"

Like a bolt the falcon shot downward.

"She strikes! She strikes!"

Tor could almost feel the heavy thud as the falcon struck her quarry. Feathers floated in the air, and the pheasant plummeted to earth, not to move again.

Argon ran to where the pheasant lay as the falcon returned, luring her back to his wrist with a tidbit.

Tor hurried on, still trying to catch up with the hunt. The Queen and her party were riding at an easy gallop, following Argon, when something went amiss. Tor could see the horse next to the Queen's palfrey stumble and fall, throwing her rider!

"Lila!" cried Tor. "It's Lila — and Galahad!"

He ran as fast as he could, still holding the nervous goshawk.

All about lay rocks — some white, some brown, some mossy — washed up from the river or washed down from the hills. Among these the sorrel mare had missed her footing. Here the riders, including the Queen, had again dismounted and were standing or kneeling about Galahad. Rimbot was running to join these.

Lila was being led to one side, dragging a foreleg. There she stood with hanging head, the brown saddle under her heaving belly.

Tor's breath caught in a sob.

"Lila! *Lila's hurt!*"

What then had happened to Galahad?

As the frightened boy reached the group. Sir Caradoc and Sir Morolt were carefully lifting Galahad to his feet. The young squire's face was pale. One of his arms hung dangling. But though he staggered between the two knights, he went to the little suffering mare and took her drooping head on his shoulder, comforting her. Sir Lionel ran his hand down her foreleg and then stood back, shaking his head.

"Lila must be walked back ever so slowly," Galahad said, forgetting his own pain in his concern for his mare. "Who will stay with her?"

He glanced about the company. His eyes fell on Tor, standing dejectedly, holding the goshawk and waiting for orders.

"Tor!" Galahad said, relieved. "Tor shall care for Lila."

"Nay, young sir," Argon spoke bitterly. "This boy be a poor one to trust with your horse." His cold eyes fastened on Tor in anger, and Tor knew that his anger was justified.

"Tor will take care of Lila, won't you, Tor?" Galahad's eyes were trusting.

"Aye," Tor replied in a muffled tone.

"Give the hawk to Rimbot," Argon ordered.

Tor did as he was told, and walked over to where the quivering Lila stood, her sides heaving.

It was a subdued hawking party that returned to the castle. Queen Guinevere had no desire to fly the falcon again; nor did she care to fly the goshawks. The little conies of the hills and meadows were left safe, crouching in their burrows or peeping from the covert of a bush at the cavalcade that galloped away. Galahad was helped to a seat behind Sir Bevidere. Sir Caradoc and Sir Morolt rode close on each side to catch him if he should fall. Argon, with the falcon, rode behind a huntsman; Rimbot, with both goshawks, was taken behind another.

Far behind again, Tor was left with the injured mare. As he fondled her head, Tor was dismayed to discover that Lila's headstall was unbuckled and halfway off. With a sickening sense of guilt, he realized that this again was his doing. The bridle had not held for Galahad when Lila stumbled.

Then his eyes caught sight of the saddle. The girth was loose, and the saddle turned easily in Tor's hands. This was Alin's doing. Both he and Tor had failed Galahad. And now he was hurt, and Lila, poor Lila! Tears came to Tor's eyes as he helped the suffering mare.

He talked lovingly to her as he led her, slowly hobbling around the hill and among the strewn stones that had been her undoing, across the long stretch of grassland, past the broad-spreading larch trees swaying their empty nests, skirting the marsh with its rustling spears.

Step by painful step, with many a long rest, the two went toward home and the help Lila needed so badly. It was late before the mare limped into her shed, her pretty head hanging. Worn out and troubled, Tor left her in the hands of Gorman, who had returned from Camelot. Then he went to the mews to face Argon and receive the punishment he expected. His back was sore when he went supperless to bed. But when he lay down near Rimbot, the boy smuggled a loaf into his hands.

Next morning he learned that Galahad would be some time in bed, but would get well. With his heart lighter, Tor went to Lila.

Gort and Grunden were there, following Gorman's skillful directions. Alin was sitting gloomily in the doorway, his chin on his fists, his cap over his forehead, looking out over the tiltyard. He scowled at Tor.

"Look what you've done," he said bitterly. "Lila ruined, and Galahad — " He gulped and glared at Tor.

Tor stopped short. His eyes flashed as angrily as Alin's, and his hands clenched.

"What *I've* done!"

74

"Yes, what *you've* done!" Alin jumped up. "You didn't fasten the headstall. It came unbuckled just when she stumbled — "

Tor turned pale, but his eyes did not waver.

"I know that. It was unbuckled and half off when I started to lead her back. But she didn't fall because of that. She wouldn't. You saddled her. The girth was too loose. When she stumbled, the saddle turned. If it hadn't been for you — "

Gorman stepped to the doorway and stood looking at them sternly.

"Alin," he said, "is it right for a page to quarrel with a churl? Return to the castle and tell Sir Kay that the mare is being well cared for. He will tell Galahad."

Without a word, but with another threatening glare at Tor, Alin marched away. Tor, knowing that it was time for him to help with the eyases, went slowly back to the mews. Grief and a feeling of guilt he could not banish were in his heart, but anger too smoldered there.

It was late afternoon before he saw Alin again. Going down to the moat to wash some perches, he came upon a party of pages swimming there, a practice that had been strictly forbidden at that point by Sir Kay. The smallest page, a little boy of about seven in pale blue, was sitting dolefully on a rock beside the piled clothing, watching the fun. If they left their garments unguarded, the pages were afraid that Slimshanks, the King's jester, who loved nothing better than such a prank, would contrive to steal them or throw them into the water.

Alin had come along behind Tor, although Tor had not seen the tall page. Standing on the bank, without looking at Tor, who was kneeling, Alin threw off his tunic, hose, and sandals. Before he dived, he jerked his head toward Tor.

"Watch my clothes."

Tor paid no attention to this. He would show Alin that he owed no obedience to a page. Tor rose leisurely, threw off his coarse linen shirt, and sprang into the water, striking out hand over hand toward the other side of the moat.

The small boy in blue stood up, shrieking:

"He's in the moat! The churl's in the moat!"

There were astonished yells from the other pages.

"Get out of here!"

"Duck him, Gervane!"

"Hold his head down!"

Numbers were against Tor. He headed back swiftly and climbed the muddy bank. He seized his shirt and put it on before the yelling pages came scrambling to shore. Tor turned to face them. With a rush, clothing was picked up and flung on hastily, for everybody felt that this was not the end of the incident. There was sure to be something more. Alin would never stand for such impudence. Tor waited, breathing hard. If they rushed him, he would do his best before he went down. Alin waved the others back and stepped close.

"Why didn't you watch my clothes?" he asked. "When I tell a churl what to do, I expect him to do it. Where I come from — "

"And where is that?" Tor thrust back his wet mane and stare defiantly

"My father is lord of thousands like you," retored Alin, thrusting out his chin. "If you were only a page, I'd — "

It was more than Tor could take. He struck that outthrust chin with a hard fist. Alin, being off balance, was staggered by the blow. There was a whoop from the pages.

"Give it to him, Alin!"

"Knock his head off!"

"Throw him in the moat!"

Alin came at Tor with his dark eyes blazing, all thought of knightliness forgotten.

"You — you *churl!*" he growled between his teeth, "I'll teach you!"

Tor put up a guard of fists, knowing what was

coming, hoping to block it. He believed he was as strong as the taller boy. But with his longer reach, Alin got through Tor's guard with a heavy blow that sent Tor reeling backward, his hands clutching the air. Over the muddy, slippery margin of the moat he went down into the water, his head striking a stone that jutted just below the edge of the bank. He knew nothing more for a few minutes.

Tor came to, and found himself lying face down, with someone pounding him on the back. Tor gagged and retched, vomiting water, choking. He struggled over, coughing, and sat up, gasping and spitting. In a minute he pushed back his clinging hair to look around. Alin, his clothing dripping, was still bending over him. A wet cut on the page's chin was bleeding. Around them were the other pages, staring, round-eyed and pale.

"Are you all right?" asked Alin anxiously. "I thought I'd never get the water out of you. Can you stand? Here — give me your hand; let me help you up."

At that moment the small boy in blue raised a shrill cry.

"Sir Kay's coming around the tower! Look out!"

The other pages scattered like partridges. Alin stood beside Tor. Sir Kay approached and surveyed them calmly.

CHAPTER 7

*In which Tor works
for Brok the armorer
and saves the life of
Lila's baby colt*

S IR KAY looked from Alin to Tor and back again,
from the cut on Alin's chin to Tor's fast-black-
ening eye and the growing lump on his head. He
knew — Gorman had told him — that they were
unfriendly, but he wasn't just sure that they had
been actually fighting, although he suspected it.
But they had undoubtedly both been in the moat,
and he had forbidden that.

"How does it happen that you were in the moat, Tor?"

Tor wiped his face on his arm, not looking at Alin.

Then he stood up.

"I fell in, Sir Kay," he said. "Alin pulled me out. I — I think I hit my head on something as I slipped over the bank."

Sir Kay looked at Alin, smiling a little to himself and taking his chin in his hand. Apparently neither lad was going to tell on the other. At any rate, whatever the trouble had been, it was over for now. He beckoned Alin aside and spoke to him briefly. Then Alin, whistling through his teeth, went off, swinging his shoulders, without a glance at Tor.

"It seems that you are not overbusy," said the steward, turning again to Tor. "I must find a place where your training, which the King promised your father, can go on apace. Argon tells me — " Sir Kay paused, rubbed the side of his long nose as if weighing something in his mind. Tor stood before him, the water still dripping from his shirt and hair. He was thinking apprehensively, "Argon's complained, as he threatened he would." But he waited, not speaking.

"Argon feels," went on the steward, "that a youth of eighteen or thereabout would be better to train as a falconer. So, as Brok the armorer has spoken well of you — ”

"Brok!”

Tor's heart lightened. If he could only work with the kindly, patient Brok! It would make all the difference in the world.

Sir Kay nodded gravely.

"I told him I would send you. An armorer's work is very honorable, Tor, and an armorer must be a man whose heart is in his work. Do you understand me?”

Tor flushed.

"Yes, Sir Kay. I'll — I'll have my heart in it — this time.”

Brok seemed glad to see Tor. He put his new helper to work clearing up the workbench, sorting spurs, rivets, bags of small bronze and brass plates, iron rings, and links, lengths of chain, and such things, so that his hands and his head would become acquainted with them. Tor liked to handle them. He felt that here at last was the place he liked best of all. As he worked, he made up his mind that he would become an armorer. Perhaps someday he might even be trusted to work on armor for King Arthur, as Brok did. Tor began to whistle cheerfully.

Shields, round or oval or pointed, all strongly

made of wood or thicknesses of hide and rimmed with iron, spiked and bossed, all light and tough, stood along the walls and hung on pegs. Javelins and jousting lances lay on racks or shelves. Brok showed Tor three helmets in a case: one of the square kind many knights preferred, one made of leather with strips of metal, and the third a Saxon helmet, cone-shaped and with a straight nosepiece down the front.

There was much to learn — even more, Tor decided, than there was at the falconer's. Every day he worked with a will, hammering, caring for the charcoal brazier, holding pieces of armor or iron in the tongs while Brok hammered, learning to make rivet holes and to shape chain links. There were unending jobs to do. Even the tiniest link or plate or rivet was so important, so much a part of the safety of a knight, that Tor realized more and more what Sir Kay had meant. This was honorable work, responsible work, and he would put his heart into it.

The boy had time — for Brok and Brok's good wife saw to that — to visit Lila, to brush her and talk to her, to lay his fingers on the white star on her forehead, telling her how sorry he was about her fall. Her leg seemed slow in getting well, and the beautiful mare often stood with her eyes half closed and her head down. But she always nuzzled

Tor's shoulder and ate from his hands the clover he pulled for her.

After visiting a little while with the mare, Tor would sometimes go to visit the kennels. He would race in the meadow with Bolar and the barking, frisking dogs, and pet and talk to old Agricola, and sometimes stop for a little while to watch the tilting. But he was always back at the workbench when Brok expected him. Occasionally, when the boy wasn't looking, the armorer would glance at him kindly and, plying his awl or lacing his thongs, would nod to himself as if he were well pleased.

One day Brok took the finished hauberk, all glittering in the sunshine, across the bailey to the castle armory. When he returned, he began work on one for Sir Launcelot.

The bent little armorer worked awhile in silence, but finally, handing Tor a buckle to polish, told him a bit of news he had gathered at the castle.

"Sir Launcelot is off on another mission. A little maid called Nimue came to the King, beseeching a champion to save her sister. The sister's husband and many another knight have been thrown into a dungeon by a wicked knight, the giant Caulang of the Marshes. Nimue's sister is imprisoned in her own castle.

"Sir Launcelot was still weary from his last mission, yet nothing would please him but that he go on this one. The little maid's tears were too much for King Arthur, and he gave Launcelot leave to go. Methinks it would better have been Sir Morodoc or Sir Gervaine, or some other who was fresh. But truly Caulang is a fearsome foe, and even the greatest knight in all Britain will find him hard to defeat."

Brok finished what he was doing and picked up another piece of work before he went on with his news.

"The King intends to make Galahad a knight soon. The young squire is only fifteen, but tall and strong. I ween he will be as brave and gentle a champion as his father, Sir Launcelot."

Tor thought of the last day he had watched Galahad tilting at the quintain. Galahad had struck the helmet fairly, but his lance had splintered and he had thrown it away, saying that he would have to get another for the next time.

"Brok," asked Tor, "could I learn to make a lance for Galahad?"

The armorer was twirling the swivel of a falcon's lunys.

"It would be a long, hard job. It would mean much work."

"I know. But — if I could only do it — to make up for something I didn't do — "

Brok thought awhile.

"I had the finest piece of ash wood, straight of

grain, tough and well-seasoned — the finest I ever saw — out in the pile beside the shop. But it took fire and is charred."

Tor hung his head. That's what he got for his forgetting — his failure to obey orders. Oh, if he had only been able to save that one piece!

"Perhaps," Brok was saying, "you might happen to find a bit of ash wood somewhere in the woods."

The next day, with his master's permission, Tor went down to the woodward to ask about ash wood.

It was the woodward's job to know the paths and dells, the deer tracks and hare warrens of the woods, the best pools of river and lake, the ripest trees to be cut for logs, the wild fruits growing here and there, the game in the marshes, the hollow trees in which the little wild bees had their hives, and many another thing. He walked much through the woods, a sling in his belt and a bow over his shoulder — a slow, silent man who cared little for castle folk or for his neighbor villagers, but loved the quiet forest and the streams. He stood half listening to Tor's questions, looking away through the branches.

"Not a seasoned piece do I know of save one I saw at Wendo's hut as I passed yesterday. Now I must away to the forest. Go you to the charcoal burner, Tor."

But when Tor, out of breath, reached the hut of the wrinkled and blackened little churl, Wendo said that he had just burned the ash wood. Sadly giving up all hope of making the lance, and blaming himself bitterly, Tor stopped on his way back to talk with Father Kent.

"Sit down, my son," said the hermit. "It pleasures my old eyes to see you."

"It — it pleasures me too."

Tor sat down and watched the old man prepare his fish. After he had it well wrapped in leaves and lying among the hot ashes, Father Kent went to the back of his cave and came out dragging a length of ash wood.

"Here is what you have been wishing for, my son," he said. "Do your best to make it, and you will succeed."

"Where — where did you — how did you —" stammered Tor. "Oh, I'm glad to have it, Father Kent. I'll try to make a good one."

"It is well," said Father Kent. "Now let us have food and drink together before you return to the castle."

Slowly the lance took shape, Brok giving careful instructions. It must be thick at the lower end, with a hollow for the arm and a bell-like thickening in front of this to give strength and protection. The other lances were there for Tor to examine and copy, but the tough, light, seasoned ash Father Kent had given him was — he thought to himself, not telling Brok — like Galahad himself, sound and true. Tor worked hard, obeying Brok's directions carefully, measuring, cutting, whittling, rasping, polishing. The taper, gradual and smooth, was the hardest to make perfect. It took a good eye, a careful, patient hand, and many measurements. The point must be but a thumb's breadth through.

Brok was patient too. He would leave his work on helmet or shield and take the lance from Tor, balance it, squint along it with one eye shut, measure it, and then, giving his advice, hand it back.

"A knight trusts his life to his lance, Tor. Right careful must you be to a hair's breadth in the scraping. Turn it and turn it again, balance, and sight. Go slowly. Watch every streak of graining. If a flaw be found that you cannot scrape or polish away, the lance may as well be thrown on the fire. It will prove a traitor, like an untrustworthy knight, to him who depends on it."

As he bent over the springy shaft lovingly, Tor thought that the life of Galahad might one day be saved by this lance. For that he would grudge no care or patience or labor. Early and late he toiled on the weapon.

Making the lance head was easier, for Tor had

already learned something about heating the iron and hammering it while it was red. Brok was willing to hold the reddened iron in the tongs and tell him where and how to strike, and, if he made a mistake, to show him how to correct it.

Then at last came the putting of the head on the shaft, another particular piece of work. If the lance head were to come off in combat, the lance would be a traitor to Galahad. The tapered end must fit exactly into the hole in the iron head; the head must be heated just right when it went on — not too cold, for it would not be tight enough; not too hot, for it would ruin the point. It must be just hot enough so that, fitted snugly over the end, it would shrink in cooling and grip the ash wood until a man could neither pull nor knock it off.

One day, when all these things had been done, the lance was finished. Brok took it, ran his hand over the entire length, feeling for the least fine hint of roughness, examined the lance head and the curve for the arm, and at last, drawing down his brows and looking at the anxious Tor, nodded approval.

"Is it — do you think it's — " Tor hesitated, his eyes on Brok's quiet face.

"Fit for a king's hand," answered Brok soberly. "The King himself would be proud to have it, if you chose to offer it to him. He would reward you well for it."

Tor took the lance silently and stood it on end, the lance head reaching away up into the far corner of the shed roof. His eyes traveled along its length. It seemed strange to think that he had really made it. He wished his father and mother — and Bren and Blaize and the others — could see it. He thought of King Arthur, with his golden helmet on, the dragon crest above it, and his glittering hauberk. Brok had said this lance was good enough for the King.

Tor shook his head.

"I made it for Galahad, Master," he said, "and nobody else."

Galahad was still recovering, and had not been out of the castle. So Tor put the lance high up on pegs. When Galahad was knighted, then would be the time for the gift.

Late that day, when Tor went for a visit with Lila, Grunden was cleaning the shed. The mare was standing holding her weight on three legs, as the hurt foreleg was stiff with bandages. Tor straightened her forelock and brought her a drink, which she took thirstily. But she would not touch the clover he brought.

"Has Gorman been here?" Tor asked.

The churl grunted.

"Him? Not for three days. Gort says he was sent to the Vale of Avalon. Gort and me's been tending the beast here. Gort knows a wonderful lot — charms and such he got from his grandmother."

"Well then, she must be all right," said Tor a little anxiously.

The churl spat.

"Sure as little fish! She be waiting for her colt — and Beltran's. The young un will be coming along soon."

Tor thought a good deal about the mare that night, recalling how hot her head had felt when he laid his cheek against it and how dull her eyes had been.

"She almost didn't know me. I wish Gorman hadn't been sent away."

At daybreak Tor went quickly toward the hackney stables. Grunden was coming out of Lila's shed with a jug of water. The lean little churl looked cross and sleepy, jerked his tousled head, and went out into the tiltyard to empty the jug. Tor went in. Gort was stooping over a small dark creature in a corner.

"Lila!" cried Tor. "She — "

" 'Tis the colt. A weak little beast, seeming."

Lila had lain down, the first time since she had been hurt. Gort stepped past the colt and went out.

Tor knelt to look at the little colt. A tiny, dark

90

thing it was, with baby hoofs and bits of ears soft to touch. The little creature was small and helpless, and yet it would likely be a great black war charger like its handsome sire.

Lila seemed half asleep. Tor murmured to her gently:

"You have a little baby colt, Lila. Are you glad?"

She moved her head, and her ears pricked forward. Tor smoothed her neck and went on talking about the colt.

"He'll be big and black, Lila. He'll make you look like a little horse beside him when he's grown. You'll be proud of him. Galahad will ride him when he's a knight."

Tor got up and began to tidy the floor, moving carefully, still talking to the mare. He did not leave her until the two churls, having had breakfast, came back.

Not until noon did he have a chance to return to the shed. Gort and Grunden were still there, looking gloomily at Lila. She was struggling unsuccessfully to get up. But the strained foreleg and the wrenched shoulder would not do their part in lifting her. She would try and try, and then, with a queer sound like a groan, sink back.

"Little un has had no milk," Grunden said to Tor. "We be waiting till Gorman comes back. He'll know how to get the mare up."

"But the colt! He'll starve. Can't we do something?"

Gort looked around, frowning.

"I made a fire of straw in the tiltyard and threw in three hairs of his tail, saying something I know will help. It'll have to do. If there was another mare with a colt, I'd take him to her. But ain't none. Gorman ought to be back tonight. Grunden, we've work to do. Come along."

The two churls went out. Tor stepped to the door and stared helplessly after them. They were leaving the colt with nothing to keep it from starving. It could not reach its mother, nor could she help. She struggled vainly to rise and then sank down.

Tor went to the door and stood looking out vaguely. He didn't know how to get Lila up. Her baby needed milk, warm mother's milk. If it didn't get that, it would die. Tor felt a mist in his eyes and an ache in his breast. Lila's little colt, and Beltran's, to die! Perhaps Lila even! She was feverish and suffering. Gort had said her udder was sore.

His mind went to the dun heifer. It was nothing to her to have a calf. Why couldn't Lila — worth so much more — why couldn't she have her baby as safely? The answer was clear. Lila had been hurt. His doing — and Alin's.

He stood very still, but a thought was striking through his pain and worry like a swift sickle through a tangle of weeds. If he could bring the heifer up to the colt, perhaps it would save him! Tor ran out and started toward the postern gate. No one was in the tiltyard. Pages, squires, and hackneys were all down the river practicing horsemanship in a larger space. As he got to the gate, Tor remembered something. He must not go without asking Brok. He turned and ran back to the armorer's. Hearing the story, Brok approved and told him to go.

Down in the valley, Tor didn't take time to hunt for his father, but hurried out into the meadow to drive the little dun heifer, with her calf behind her, out of the field, along the woods road, and at last up the hill.

Leaving Spotty and the bull calf in the tiltyard, empty of youths and horses still, he hurried to the shed. Nobody was there, he knew, for he had called out as he passed. Lila lay as he had left her, and on his truss of straw was the little colt, his legs stretched out and his eyes closed.

Tor seized a jug and went out to milk what was left in the heifer's udder. It wasn't much. Spotty's calf had taken most of it. Still there was need for only a little.

He set the wide-mouthed jug close to the colt, put his fingers into the warm milk, and pressed them into the small lips. The colt struggled to his feet and stood wobbling, his long weak legs spread. He was a pitiful sight.

"Poor little un! Try this. Suck my fingers; try again."

It was slow. The hungry little creature sucked greedily, but he was getting almost nothing. Tor wished he had something the colt could really suck from. He sat back on his heels, scratching his head, looking anxiously from the colt to the jug. Then he remembered the leathern bottles, and dashed out and across to the cookhouse to borrow one.

Tearing a strip from his tunic, Tor soaked it in the milk, poured the milk into the bottle, stoppered it with the dripping rag, and tilted it to the colt's lips. The little creature began to suck eagerly. Tor braced the bottle and held the rag. Finally the colt was getting a meal. As the last of the warm milk disappeared, the door squeaked and Alin stepped inside.

"Why didn't somebody tell Galahad?" he asked. "He didn't know a thing about Lila's being this way. Why didn't you come for me? I'd have told him, and he'd have — "

"Because I was too busy trying to save the colt. I had to go down to the village."

"If you had time to go to the village, you had time to find me. I was nearer than the village."

"If I *had* found you and you had gone to tell

Galahad, the little colt might have been too weak to save. Lila's sick and feverish and sore, and can't get up on account of her shoulder. When Gorman comes — "

"It all sounds crazy to me. Here, give me that bottle. What's in it?"

"Nothing — now!"

Alin glanced at the bottle disgustedly.

"Well if you're silly enough to be giving him morat — "

"I'm not."

"Galahad told me to look after the colt," Alin said. "Gorman's back and coming right over. I know something about horses. My father — "

"Then why didn't you tighten the saddle as you should have?" asked Tor hotly. "Look what you did to Lila. Did you tell that to Galahad?"

Alin threw down the bottle and clenched his fists.

"And perhaps you'll tell Galahad how you left the bridle unbuckled so he couldn't control her when she stumbled. A fine one you are to have charge of Lila's colt! If it hadn't been for you, Lila would be all right — and so would Galahad."

There was the sound of footsteps at the door.

CHAPTER 8

*In which Tor is dismissed
from Camelot Castle by Sir
Kay, and Queen Guinevere's
white falcon is lost*

WITH Gorman looking over his shoulder, Sir
Kay the steward stood in the doorway. The
faces of both men were stern. The knight stepped
in and stood looking a minute at Lila and then at
the colt, now sound asleep, stretched out near his
mother. Lila had given up struggling to get up.
Even in his confusion, Tor felt glad that the men
had come at last. Now Lila would have the help

she needed; they would manage to get her up, and she would be able to feed her colt.

The steward's face was severe as he turned toward Tor.

"Is it true what I just heard Alin say? Did you leave the bridle unbuckled, or was he mistaken?"

Tor swallowed.

"I — I — "

"Did you?"

"Yes, Sir Kay."

Tor glanced at Alin, whose dark face had reddened. The page turned uncertainly toward the door. Sir Kay beckoned to the waiting Gorman.

"Gorman," he said, "you take care of the mare. Alin will help you. Better send for Gort and Grunden. If Lila can stand, she can manage to feed her colt. Until she can, the young cow in the meadow out there will help. Tor, come outside."

Tor followed. Alin moved aside to let him pass, but did not look at him. Tor thought:

"Alin isn't going to tell about the saddle!"

He could hardly believe it. Alin surely wasn't a coward! Alin was a page, and one day would be a knight. He — he was just waiting.

Sir Kay walked a little way from the shed and stood looking down at Tor, frowning.

"I have given you several chances, Tor," he said

at last. "But I have come to realize that you will not make good. I don't know why I expected it. Go home. Tell your father I am sorry his boon turned out so badly."

Tor did not answer. He stood looking up at the steward almost as if he had not understood. His thoughts were confused. Lila! He wouldn't see Lila! The colt would grow and play — and — somebody else would be with it. Brok — what would Brok say? The lance! Could he give it to Galahad now? A recreant knight — would he be like a recreant knight? He hardly heard Sir Kay.

"Tell your good father from me that you are sent home because you have been found untrustworthy."

The tall steward turned and went back into the shed, while Tor, looking neither right nor left, went across the bailey, past the tiltyard where the quintain, battered by many a lance thrust, seemed to glare at him, muttering:

"Untrustworthy! Untrustworthy!"

He went out by the postern, crossed the moat by the footbridge, and plodded down the hillside among the bushes and small trees. When he got to the riverbank, he sat down on a stone and looked into the water a long time. He was hardly thinking; his mind was a confused mixture of images rather than thoughts. Lila. Her colt. Galahad. The lance. He stood up and threw a pebble into the water. He knew he must go home and — and tell his father and mother.

It was a long time before he could walk to the village and the field where he knew his father would be.

When he told Wain what Sir Kay had said, the cowherd listened without speaking, and as silently to Tor's explanations. He saw Tor's faults, but he saw other things too, which would be virtues even in a knight: boldness, kindness, truthfulness. But Wain was not a man to say many things. All he did was to put his large brown hand on Tor's shoulder and say:

"It is not so bad to be a village man, my son. A churl may be noble as a king, if he so wills it. Forget this matter of knights and pages. Go into the forest. Take Fag and hunt birds' nests. I'll make it all right with your mother. Come back home with the setting of the sun. Tomorrow you shall go into the far oak wood with Fag and Ron and Swithin, and help with the swine. It will be best."

With the joyous Fag beside him, Tor went into the woods, going a long way around to avoid meeting anyone from the village. He didn't care about birds' nests, but just walked aimlessly, sometimes sitting on a fallen log, when Fag would come and frolic in front of him. Gradually he went farther and farther from the village, past the charcoal burner's little hut, along the stream from the hermit's cave.

As he sat down to rest, he thought he heard the tinkle of a bell. He started and looked all around. Fag had jumped up and begun to bark, looking up into a tree, wagging his tail violently, and mixing excited little yelps with the barks. Tor ran to the tree and looked up. It was from up there that the bell tinkled — a bell like the ones the falcons wore. But how could a belled falcon be up in the tree?

There was a threshing about among the branches at the tree's top. Tor began climbing as fast as he could, stopping now and then to peer upward. At last he caught sight of a large white bird with flailing wings, and with feet tangled in straps that were caught among the branches.

"The gerfalcon!" Tor breathed, his excitement mounting. "She's got away from the mews somehow. Oh, if I can only catch her and take her back!"

Fag's yelping was frightening the falcon, but Tor could not quiet the excited dog. Tor gripped the trunk of the giant beech with legs and arms, finding footing here and there on limbs reaching outward, scrambling up to others. The gerfalcon was in the topmost part of the tree where the boughs were not so thick through. Tor wondered whether they would bear his weight that far up. He looked down. The ground was a long way off. Fag, panting, had sat down and was looking up with his tongue hanging out.

At length, groping among the clustering leaves, Tor found his way to a limb that led up and out toward the struggling gerfalcon. He pulled off some of the leaves and rested, looking around to plan what he could do. The bird was still threshing with her beautiful barred white wings, hanging head downward. Tor knew that one stroke of those flailing pinions might make him fall from the tree. He must be careful. Fortunately the gerfalcon, her eyes closed by the seeling cord, could not see him. If he could manage to reach her and loosen the lunys —

He began to edge carefully up and outward. This limb had few side branches; some of these looked dead and half rotten. Inch by inch he must pick his way. If he trusted his weight to a half-rotten limb, he would fall. Then who was to get the gerfalcon — the finest in all Britain — the Queen's own bird? She might get loose, with all this struggling, at any minute.

The boughs were swaying dangerously under his feet. He was forced to grip tightly and step back, realizing that, stretch as far as he could, he could not reach the struggling falcon.

He propped himself in a crotch to think. Even supposing that he could take hold of the bird, she would bite his hand so fiercely with her strong curved beak that he would not be able to hold her while keeping his balance and dodging the beating of her wings. But there had to be some way. He looked along the limb that was bending and swaying with the heavy falcon's struggles.

"If I could only manage to break it off," he thought, "she'd fall. But — it might ruin her."

He inched along again, gripping the limb with his knees, leaning forward. The threshing of her wings helped him as he timed his efforts against the dry wood where the lunys held. Gathering all his strength, he strained and pulled. There was a crack and a crash. The wood had splintered and was falling down, down, down through the leaves, striking against the spreading branches, while the gerfalcon swirled, flapping her wings and catching vainly at the branches with her beak and talons.

Tor scrambled downward as fast as he dared, yelling to Fag, whose barking was mad with excitement.

"Down, Fag! Down!"

As he neared the bottom, Tor found that the bird was again held fast. This time the branch on which she was caught was wedged in a crotch. But he could reach her now, or — what was safer — reach the end of the branch and lift her, still dangling by the lunys, free of the crotch.

It was hard to lower the big bird from limb to limb, wedge the branch here and there until he could manage his foothold, and then get her farther down. But at last he came to the lowest limb from which he had to drop, holding the broken piece, trying to keep it high so that the big bird would not be hurt against the ground.

He landed on his back. When he scrambled to his feet he saw the gerfalcon struggling on the ground, the branch jerked about among the trees and bushes. Fag, insane with excitement, was unable to reach her because of wings and beak.

"Down, Fag! Down!"

He could lift the branch to his shoulder now and hurry away through the woods with the big hawk dangling behind him. He wondered if the gerfalcon was ruined, but as far as he could see, though her feathers were badly rumpled and she was very frightened and angry, she was not hurt.

At the hut of Wendo the charcoal burner, he

found that the sooty churl had just cooked himself a dish of stewed eels. Nothing could have been better. Tor managed to quiet the bird and to feed her. Then he fashioned a sort of perch and fastened her comfortably on it, so that he could carry her right side up. This done, he set out for the castle, with Wendo's last words echoing in his mind.

"They'll be main glad to see you with the big hawk, Tor!"

Up to now Tor had not thought of it, but perhaps Wendo was right. They would be glad. He could almost hear Sir Kay or the King saying, "You have done well and bravely, Tor. Come back and live at the castle again!"

He quickened his steps. He could hardly wait to get there. His face was flushed, his heart beating high with hope. This would make up for everything. They would forgive him and let him try again!

At the foot of the hill Rimbot broke through the trees, his freckled face pale, his eyes wild and frightened. When he caught sight of Tor and the gerfalcon, Rimbot stopped and stared, trembling and gasping for breath.

"Oh, Tor! You found her! Now it will be all right. I'll have her back and quieted before the Master gets back."

"How did she get away?"

"It was when I was mending the lunys. She flew up and wouldn't come back. If you hadn't found her — I — I'd have had to run away. I don't know what Argon would have done. Half killed me, I think."

Tor's heart sank. Recovering the Queen's falcon meant so very much to Rimbot. But it meant much to Tor also. It wasn't fair that he should lose this chance of making up for his failures after all his hard struggle to save the precious falcon. As these thoughts crowded into his mind, Tor remembered seeing Rimbot's bruised back, and remembered too his own sore back the day of the hawking.

Rimbot reached out his leather-covered wrist. His face pale, Tor gave up the handsome white bird. Rimbot turned to start up the hill, calling back to Tor:

"Come on, Tor. Hurry!"

Tor shook his head. "I'll stay down here," he said steadily. "You go on, Rimbot. I'm glad I found her for you."

The falconer's helper went on as fast as he could go, his round face full of joyful relief. Tor turned slowly back toward home. He could never go back to the castle now — never. His last chance was gone.

CHAPTER 9

*In which Tor aids
Sir Launcelot and
is allowed to return
to Camelot Castle*

THE days went slowly by as Tor slipped back into his old life among the churls of the village. He tried not to think too often of the beautiful mare, wondering how her leg was, or picture to himself the colt nuzzling at her flank. Bren had gone up and driven Spotty and her calf home. He said the mare was doing well and the colt thriving.

Every morning Tor and Fag went with Ron and Swithin to herd the swine, and at sunset they came home.

One day Swithin sent Tor back to the village for a drinking horn. As he was returning, the sound of a crash came from an open glade not far from the hermit's cave. There were hoarse and muffled shouts, and then the thunder of hoofbeats followed by more crashes and loud yells. Tor tried to get through a thicket to see what was happening. But seeing, he crouched back in the shelter of the bushes.

A gigantic man in a black hauberk and helmet, astride the largest horse Tor had ever seen, was just in front of him. Some distance down the glade, where the sunshine fell directly upon him, a knight lay motionless on the ground, the scales of his hauberk shining like silver. His shield lay where it had fallen, and the cause of his downfall, a splintered lance, was not far away, the point sticking upright in the turf. Near by stood a coal-black war horse, his head up in fright, his nostrils flaring as he snorted.

The giant in front of Tor was getting heavily off his horse. When he had dismounted, he drew his sword and started toward the fallen knight. It was at that moment that Tor recognized Beltran.

It was the gallant Launcelot who lay like one dead; his untrustworthy lance had failed him!

Shivering in the thicket, Tor knew that the giant would take the knight prisoner to some dark dungeon and hold him for ransom, taking his armor and his horse as well. Or it might be even worse than that. As the giant, who must be the terrible Caulang, went toward the fallen Launcelot, the sound of a distant horn came from within the woods. The giant stopped, listened a minute, and then, clumsily remounting, put spurs to his horse. With a thunder of heavy hoofs that seemed to shake the wood, the big animal galloped away, Caulang holding his lance ready for an attack.

Tor ran forward and knelt beside Sir Launcelot. He tried to arouse the unconscious knight, but could not. What could he do? Caulang would be coming back. Tor looked around for help. There was no one to tell him what to do. He must think, and think fast. On the ground the leaves of last autumn lay in swirls and mounds, many caught in the thickets. If he could only hide Sir Launcelot — hide him and cover him with leaves! Then Caulang couldn't harm him.

His plan forming while he tugged, Tor dragged and rolled the heavy knight down the slant of the glade toward the river and a thicket growing there.

At last he reached it, and managed to push and pull the unconscious man into its center and to cover him with leaves. Then he ran back to strew leaves over the marks they had left.

Beltran came near his unconscious master, sniffling and snorting. Tor looked up, frightened. If Caulang saw Beltran, he would know Sir Launcelot was somewhere near. He would hunt and find him.

"Beltran! Beltran! Wait for me!"

The charger eyed Tor with flashing eyes, pawed the ground.

"Let me up, Beltran!"

Knowing Tor, Beltran let him mount and tuck his feet into the straps above the stirrups. Tor had never ridden a horse except Agricola, but now he must ride Beltran. He must get to the castle and bring help for Sir Launcelot. If the charger had gone when Caulang came back, the giant would follow the tracks, leaving the knight safely hidden. Given a start, Beltran with only a boy on his back, ought to outdistance the heavy steed carrying the huge Caulang in armor. Feeling these things, almost without thinking them, Tor settled himself in the saddle, a high pommel before him and a straight cantle behind that reached up as far as his waist. He struck his heels against Beltran's sides and turned him along the bank of the stream.

"I'll call out to Father Kent. He can go and help Sir Launcelot when Caulang's gone again."

Horse and boy had not gone far before he saw Father Kent hurrying through the woods. The little maid who had ridden away with Sir Launcelot was following the hermit. Tor shouted:

"Father Kent! Wait. Sir Launcelot — "

"I know, I know," said the old man, waving his hand. "Fear not, but ride on. Tell them at the castle that Sir Launcelot will be taken care of. The little Nimue and I will attend him. Haste! Away!"

Tor had been as quick as he could, but already much time had passed.

"Go, Beltran! Go!"

Obediently, the charger broke into a trot that threw his rider up and down until he had to clutch the pommel to keep his seat. But he shouted at the horse and kicked when he could. Beltran broke into a gallop, threading his way among the trees and bushes by his own good sense.

As Tor regained his balance, he guided the big animal into glades he knew, where the trees stood farther apart and the way led in the direction of the road past the village. He had not long left Father Kent and Nimue before he heard a hoarse, roaring shout and a crashing among the underbrush. He knew Caulang could not have seen him, but must have come on Beltran's tracks or heard the sound of his galloping hoofs.

Tor began to swing the strap that was hanging to the rein back and forth against the charger's flanks. Excited by the sounds of pursuit, the spirited war horse bounded forward at full speed. Jerking, panting, and bouncing, Tor hung to the high-peaked saddle, the reins clutched in one fist, Beltran's flying black mane whipping his face. Agricola had never been like this! Thoroughly aroused and out of hand, Beltran raced out of the woods and along the road.

Tor did not see his father and Bren in the field driving the sheep to the fold, nor even hear their shouts of amazement and fright. As the big charger dashed up the steep road, losing some of his mad speed, Tor managed to take a swift look behind. Just emerging from the forest was Caulang.

The giant rose in his stirrups, brandishing his lance, bellowing with rage. He knew he had been somehow outwitted, but sure of capturing the valuable war horse and the boy who had fooled him, he struck spurs into his steed.

Both horses had to lose speed in breasting the steep hill. When Caulang reached the bottom, Tor was not more than halfway to the top. Caulang shouted again. The big bay, his mouth foaming, his

111

nostrils wide and red, leaped forward mightily. Tor's only hope now was that the drawbridge might still be down.

In another moment, clinging, jerking from side to side, he caught sight of the bridge. Fear clutched his heart as he realized that he was too late. The sun had just sunk in a flaming sky against which the wall and towers stood tall and forbidding. According to custom, the warders were raising the drawbridge for the night.

There was no time for Tor to think, nothing more he could do. He could neither wave his hands nor, breathless and shaken as he was, shout for help, even if he could have been heard. He could only cling desperately as the excited charger bounded straight up and on toward the rising bridge and the steep bank of the moat.

Suddenly the rise of the bridge was halted. The warders had recognized the steed of Sir Launcelot and espied the giant in pursuit. The heavy bridge hung a long moment suspended, then began creaking slowly downward. Tor caught another flying glimpse of Caulang close behind him as Beltran, his hoof beats echoing, thundered across and into the castle bailey.

As Beltran left the bridge, the big bay was all but upon it when the straining and shouting warders, working at wheel and pulley, raised it beyond his reach. The giant's charger reared under the spurring that urged him to leap upon the rising timbers, whirled, and almost fell back upon his rider. The drawbridge creaked slowly to the top, as the warders and knights and squires, running to the walls, shouted defiance.

Raging, Caulang put his horn to his mouth and blew an angry blast, a mortal challenge to King Arthur and all his knights. Then, doubtless thinking of searching for the knight he had lost, he did not wait for an answer, but rode swiftly down the hill and disappeared in the woods.

There was great excitement in the bailey. A squire was sent with Beltran to the stables. Sir Kay brought Tor before the King to tell his story. The King listened gravely.

"You have done bravely and well, Tor," he said, speaking almost as Tor had dreamed he would the day he had saved the falcon. "A brave and knightly deed have you done. Ask any fitting boon and by my halidom, it will not be denied!"

They were in Queen Guinevere's tiring room. Arthur sat in a carved chair near the Queen, and ladies and pages stood about, the colors of tunics and robes gay against the soft tints of tapestries. Tor looked at the King.

"If — if I could come back!" he said. "If I could come back and work with Brok — "

Puzzled, the King glanced at Sir Kay. The steward stood holding his white wand before him, looking uncertainly at Tor. Arthur looked at the boy too, a wrinkle coming between his brows. Queen Guinevere pressed her hand against the King's shoulder and spoke kindly.

"Why had you gone back to the village, young Tor?"

Tor stirred uncomfortably.

"I — I was sent home," he faltered, "because I — "

He could not go on, but pressed his knuckles against his lips and stood looking wordlessly into Guinevere's face.

Both Arthur and Guinevere turned inquiringly to Sir Kay.

The steward's voice was grave as he stepped forward to explain.

"My lord King, the boy was given work to do, according to the boon granted his good father, Wain the headman. But, though I am sorry to have to say it, Tor proved disobedient and untrustworthy. I tried him again and again, for I felt a kindness for the bold lad. When at last it appeared that the laming of Galahad's mare and the fall of

Galahad were his fault, I sent him back to his father."

There was a moment's silence. The eyes of all those in the tiring room were upon Tor. Feeling this, he stiffened and looked straight ahead, for what could he say? King Arthur looked disappointed. Galahad started swiftly forward from his station beside the door and kneeled before the King.

"Speak, Galahad," said the King. "For the saving of brave Sir Launcelot, any fitting boon must and shall be granted. Speak."

"Lord Arthur," answered Galahad boldly, "it is right that Sir Launcelot's son should speak for Tor. He is bold and brave and kind. As for Lila, and my accident —"

There was a queer choking sound as Alin came forward and threw himself on his knee beside Galahad.

"What? Another petitioner?" said the Queen. "My lord Arthur, this lad has good friends, it seems."

Alin's dark face, usually so arrogant, was flushed and humble.

"My lord King, it was not Tor who should have been sent away!"

Arthur leaned forward.

"What is this you say, Alin?"

Alin raised his troubled eyes.

"It was more my fault than Tor's."

Galahad turned to look into Alin's face as the page stumbled on.

"I wasn't careful enough that morning. It was my fault the saddle turned."

King Arthur raised his eyebrows, his hand fingering the golden chain on his breast.

"It turned then?" he asked of Galahad.

Galahad bowed his head.

"It turned, after the bridle failed me."

Sir Kay moved a step nearer, his calm gray eyes on Alin, waiting, like the others. Pages and damsels were silent, listening. Tor's hands were opening and closing at his sides. Alin would tell the truth at last! A flood of happiness surged over him, as much for Alin as for himself. The page was going on steadily, his eyes never leaving those of the King. It seemed as if Alin must rid himself of something that had lain heavy on him.

"The quarreling — Sir Kay didn't mention it, my lord. It was my fault too. But — I *liked* Tor under it all. But, Galahad — it seemed to me that a churl — "

"Go on," said King Arthur, sternly.

Alin's cheeks flushed painfully.

"It seemed to me that a churl — " he repeated, and gulped. "But now it's all different. I don't think — I'll never think again about Tor's being only a churl. He might have told Sir Kay about the saddle when I didn't. He might have told when I knocked him into the moat — "

Sir Kay's eyes widened, and he made a slight sound. But Alin went on unheeding.

"I stood by and let Sir Kay send him home. I was ashamed, but I didn't speak. I haven't been happy since. I pray you to let Tor come back. I'd like to be friends with him."

The two boys glanced at each other and then looked away. But Alin hadn't said all he wished to say:

"And it was Tor saved Lila's colt. He went and brought up a little cow when the colt was starving and nobody around to help. When I got to the shed that day, I saw him giving the colt something out of a leathern bottle. It was milk, cow's milk, but he didn't tell me. I didn't know till afterward."

Galahad, who had risen, put his hand on Tor's shoulder and looked anxiously at the King. Arthur nodded.

"The boon you ask — forgiveness for Tor — and the one he asks for himself — to come and work again with Brok — are both right willingly granted."

Tor's heart was full of happiness. His blue eyes met Alin's dark ones. There was no longer pride and superiority in the page's glance, but only warmth and friendship. Galahad looked from one to the other, smiling.

Sir Kay came up behind them.

"Get you off to Brok, Tor, lest I send you home again!"

But even the grave steward was smiling as he spoke.

CHAPTER 10

*In which Tor sees Sir
Launcelot and the
terrible Caulang engage
in fearsome combat*

THE next morning Tor was awakened at the
rising of the sun by a furious blowing of the
warders' trumpets. The bailey was beginning to
swarm with half-wakened yeomen and churls as he
ran out. What could have happened?

Here was Alin racing to meet him, and Tor followed the tall page up a long winding stairway to
the top of the highest tower of Camelot Castle.

Spread out below them and the knights, yeomen, and squires already thronging the battlements, was the wide view of vale and forest, lake and winding river, towered city and thatched village, all lying peacefully in the rosy glow of morning. But it was not on this that they gazed.

Before the castle the massive bay charger of the giant stood pawing and snorting; on his back was Caulang.

As the boys looked, the giant raised his trumpet to blow a long and defiant blast. Then he shook the horn in one hand, glaring up at the knights on the towers.

"Come out!" he bellowed. "Come out, cowards! Come out, come out if ye dare, any or all of ye, to face Caulang!"

Pages and squires shouted back. But the knights hastened down, not staying for idle boastings, knowing that King Arthur would be summoning them to his audience hall; knowing too that none might go forth in answer to this challenge without Arthur's permission.

Tor and Alin hurried down behind the angry men and wedged themselves in the audience hall to listen. Many of the knights were crowding swiftly forward to ask Arthur's permission to fight the arrogant giant. But the King, standing tall beside his chair, refused each one.

120

"This is Sir Launcelot's quarrel. I have faith that he will yet return to take up the challenge. Let no knight go forth from the castle."

The knights gathered in the bailey and on the battlements, raging bitterly at the giant's insults. But no one could say the King's decision was not just.

The churls went back to their work, wondering and grumbling, the women frightened, the men growling and boasting at what would come to Caulang. Squires and pages did not race out to the tiltyard, but ranged uneasily about bailey and castle.

Caulang disappeared after giving a final derisive blast. It was not long until he was back with two squires and several laden pack horses. Some distance from the castle walls there was a wide sunken field called the lists, used for jousting. Here Caulang's squires pitched a tall yellow pavilion. Into this they carried rich furnishings. A brown tent was put up behind the pavilion.

Where the first trees of the valley had marched over the brow of the hill and stood, fronting the field, the squires pickcted their horses and the giant's bay charger. When all this was ready, Caulang repeated his roaring defiant challenge. Then he went to sit in his tent, where he ate and drank mightily as his squires served him with flagon and trencher.

Thus the day went, and two other days like it. At dawn, at noontide, and at sunset, Caulang sounded his challenge before the castle gate, defying the King and all his knights, while King Arthur commanded them, "Wait!" and again, "Wait!"

During every spare minute Tor was with Alin on the tower. Would Sir Launcelot come? Was he killed? Would he never appear to take up the challenge and the quest that had been granted him? Tor felt in his own breast the fire that seemed to consume the knights who paced unceasingly upon the battlements.

Morning, and noon, and evening came and went. Neither Tor nor Alin, nor the King himself, who went often to the battlements, could catch a glimpse of the white plume of Sir Launcelot. Gorman had been sent down with Beltran; Caulang, standing in front of his pavilion, had thrown back his shaggy head to laugh and shout at sight of them, but had let charger and squire pass unhindered.

"Let Launcelot ride against me again if he will," he shouted. "Well does he know the might of my spear!"

Before sunset on the third day, Caulang again

mounted his war horse, ready to roar his threats and boasts, while the silent and scowling knights on every tower looked down. Suddenly Tor, his keen eyes wandering for a moment toward the forest, caught the movements of something white among the trees. He seized Alin's arm, scarcely daring to speak aloud for fear he might be wrong.

"Alin! Look! No — farther down. Did you see something white among the trees? There it is again!"

Alin stared, his hand shielding his eyes from the slant of the afternoon sunlight.

"Aye! Something white!"

"A plume! Alin, it's Sir Launcelot!"

The two boys raised a cheer.

"He's coming! Sir Launcelot! Sir Launcelot!"

Knights crowded to the parapet, shading their eyes and crying with full-throated shouts:

"Sir Launcelot! He comes! He comes! He comes!"

Alin ran to carry the word to the King. Arthur came, followed by Queen Guinevere and all the ladies and pages of the castle. All eyes were fastened on the road below.

Proudly he came, the greatest knight in all Britain, riding gallantly up the hill on the noble black charger. Stout Gorman rode alongside his stirrup.

A wild cheer went up from the castle battlements as Sir Launcelot came into view. Guinevere let flutter a long scarf at the brave champion, and Launcelot raised his lance in salute.

The contestants took up their stands on opposite sides of the lists. Then King Arthur cried to his trumpeter:

"Sound the charge!"

With the blare of the trumpet, the riders put spurs to their horses, and they charged toward each other at a gallop that seemed to shake the earth. Each man poised his lance and lifted high his shield to protect face and breast.

At the crash of lance on shield, a mighty cry went up from the towers. The great steeds snorted and stamped as the fighters clashed again and again. Trained for battle, the two horses were circling each other.

More clashes, more cries from the tower, and then there was a deathly hush as Sir Launcelot reeled in his saddle, his shield split in two by a blow from Caulang.

The lance had been struck from the giant's hand, but the fierce Caulang was drawing his sword, in the meantime urging on his horse to the charge.

Beltran kept his head toward the bay, striking with his forehoof as the other horse tried to turn and gain an opening for Caulang's thrust at the swaying Launcelot.

Tor's heart was pounding; from the corner of his eye he could see Queen Guinevere clasping her hands in terror.

But Launcelot steadied himself and, holding the remaining half of his shield before him, reined slowly backward to gain speed and power for another charge.

One of Caulang's squires ran forward with the fallen lance. Once more the King's trumpeter blew the charge.

Tor thought, "If Caulang was an honorable knight, he would throw away his own shield. Then Sir Launcelot would throw down the broken piece and all would be fair again."

Caulang, however, had no thought of knightly generosity. His lance was held ready to thrust at Sir Launcelot's ill-protected beast.

Launcelot aimed his own lance at his opponent's helmet, and struck a fair blow. The giant reeled and toppled heavily from the saddle. But even as he fell he thrust his lance, striking full on the knight's hauberk.

As the lance struck, the onlookers on the battlements held their breath, fearing to see their champion mortally wounded. But Launcelot's hauberk withstood the heavy blow, as the lance struck aside and slipped across the knight's chest. The skillful work of Brok the armorer had saved Launcelot's life.

But the force of the blow unhorsed him also. Now the two combatants faced each other on foot, drawing swords for desperate hand-to-hand battle. Blades whirled and slashed; shouts and screams from the tower filled the air.

Swords crashed against shield, harness, and helmet, and blade against flashing blade. Back and forth and around trod the two who fought so fiercely, parrying and thrusting, hacking and smiting.

A tremendous blow from Caulang struck Launcelot's half shield to the ground, and the gallant knight fell on one knee. With a bellow of triumph, the giant threw himself toward his kneeling foe.

Just as all seemed lost, Launcelot sprang to his feet and, with a quick upthrust of his sword, struck Caulang's blade from his grasp.

Now Launcelot's weapon was at the giant's throat, and Caulang was forced to his knees, pleading for mercy. Because the knights were sworn to show mercy to those that asked it, Sir Launcelot spared the wicked Caulang's life.

The trumpets blared in triumph; loud cheers came from the battlements. Tor and Alin ran with all the rejoicing throng to welcome Sir Launcelot as he rode brave Beltran across the drawbridge, just as the last rays of the sun glinted on the treetops on the other side of the forest.

King Arthur himself embraced Launcelot and led him into the castle to do him honor, followed by all the court.

Caulang, his big head hanging, was thrust into a dungeon, there to stay until his evil deeds had been undone. He must order his squires to free the husband of little Nimue's sister and all the other captives.

Truly, Tor thought, the sun had never gone down on a more glorious day.

CHAPTER 11

*In which Tor sees
Galahad become a knight,
and other important
events occur*

ALIN had brought Galahad to the door of
Brok's shop. The young squire, curious as to
why Alin had asked him to come, looked into the
shop. Tor came forward, smiling and holding the
lance out toward Galahad.

"It is for you."

Tor's face flushed as he saw the other's look of
delight. A feeling of pride was in his heart because

he had made this lance with his own hands for Galahad. He was glad, knowing that what he had worked on for so long was worthy of giving. Galahad's dark eyes were shining as he ran his strong brown hands lovingly along its length. Then he balanced and smoothed the graceful weapon, and held it against his side where his arm fitted snugly into place, swinging the point here and there, aiming it.

A crowd of pages and young squires going out to the tiltyard came across the bailey to gather around, thrusting forward to touch the lance and ask about it.

"In sooth, Brok is a master armorer!" exclaimed Hanay. "Never have I seen truer lance. I wish I had one nearly as good."

Brok, watching, chuckled, half to himself.

"I did not make it, fair squire," he said. "But I could not make a better one."

"Then another master armorer must have come," declared Hanay, stepping forward to look curiously around the shop. "Where is he?"

Galahad laid his hand on Tor's arm.

"Here is the armorer," he announced. "No knight could wish a finer lance than Tor has made."

The group stared at Tor and at the lance. That a village boy should have the skill to make a lance like this! It was more than they could understand. They shook their heads, bewildered, and gave it up. Then one shouted:

"Why do we stand here? Come to the tiltyard, Galahad, and try it on the quintain."

Galahad, holding the lance upright, shook his head.

"Not with this. It is for my first arming. I'll be watching beside it and my other arms tonight."

Galahad's last day as a squire wore on, and at last it was night. Brok and his good wife slept soundly, the door of their hut open to the soft summer night. But Tor lay wakeful, thinking. He thought of the battle; of Caulang, gone away defeated and humble; of the freeing of the giant's captives; of little Nimue and the shy glances between her and Alin; of noble Sir Launcelot and the fiery yet gentle Beltran; of Lila, whose leg was getting better slowly but surely; and of her colt, growing, fattening, learning to frisk around its mother, and learning too, Tor was sure, to know him and his hands. He thought of King Arthur of the golden hair and knightly heart, and of Queen Guinevere and how kindly she had spoken to him. All these things went across his mind like pictures. But the picture he loved most was that of Galahad accepting the lance. The youthful squire would soon be Sir Galahad, the youngest knight of King Arthur's court.

That very evening, before bedtime, when twilight darkened the bailey, Tor and Alin and Brok had sat together on the doorstep of the shop. The armorer had told them about the Round Table, sent by Queen Guinevere's father, King Leodegraunce, as a wedding present to King Arthur because it had once belonged to Arthur's father, King Uther. Brok said there was a strange magic about a seat that was always kept empty — waiting, it was said, for one most worthy to occupy it.

"It is called the Seat Perilous," said Brok dreamily, "and they do tell that the Wizard Merlin is the one who put on it a magic, moving writing. No unworthy knight dares sit in this seat, for there is a story that once an unworthy knight did so, and the ground opened up and swallowed him. But when the true knight, gentlest and bravest of all, comes, the Seat Perilous will bear his name and he shall sit there unharmed."

While they talked, they saw the flicker of torches on the outside steps leading down from the greatest tower of the castle. The three stood up to watch. A group of men were descending the stairs. Those in front carried torches; those behind, armor. The torchlight shone on a tall youth in a white mantle, who walked in the middle.

Tor laid his hand on Alin's arm.

"Is that — "

131

"Galahad," answered the page. "He is going to the chapel to watch and pray alone."

They watched the short procession until it disappeared through the postern. Then Tor said:

"The tall knight — was he Sir Launcelot?"

"Aye," said Brok sleepily. "Aye."

"I think he was carrying the lance."

"Aye."

Brok yawned. Alin stood up suddenly and stretched his long arms above his head. Then, with a brief good night, he went running across the moonlit bailey.

Now Tor was remembering the evening's talk and seeing again in his mind the men and the torches, but most of all the tall young figure in the sweeping white mantle with the flicker of torchlight upon it. They were going to the old chapel down the hill among the trees.

"There will be a light in its window now. Inside, in front of the altar of stone, Galahad will be all alone."

Something — a thought or a wish — drew Tor to his feet. He went softly out of the hut and began to run toward the postern. Everything was still except for the sound of his quick footsteps. Drifts of darkness lay beside every hut and shop, and in between, like a silver strand, the moonlight.

Across the bailey bulked the stern dark towers of the sleeping castle.

Tor let himself out the postern and crossed the moat on the footbridge. Among the grasses and bushes of the farther side, his feet found the well-worn footpath. Following it steadily down the hillside, winding in and out among the trees, bushes, and tumbled rocks, he came at length to the road that led to the city of Camelot.

Here it was easier going, and there was more light. Tor ran along until he came to a fork in the way. A narrow path led away from the road into the woods. As he turned into this track, staring toward a dark cluster of trees, he saw a flicker of reddish light from a narrow pointed window and a partly open door.

He made his way cautiously to the door and stopped, his hand upon it, asking himself:

"What am I doing here? Why did I come?"

He had no answer. He listened. There was no sound. Galahad was in there, watching before the altar. Surely it could not be wrong to go quietly inside. It would be helping Galahad guard his armor: the lance and sword, the white shield and the new hauberk, the golden spurs.

He slipped through the doorway, making no sound, standing in the shadowy chapel to look.

Galahad, his mantle like snow in the light of the torch, was kneeling before the altar, his sword held out between his two hands.

Tor slid gently to the stone floor. After a while, slipping farther, he put his head on his arm with a sigh. He did not wake when another figure slipped through the door, stood a few moments in the dimness, and then lay down.

The first light of the morning sunshine came through this doorway that faced the east. Aroused, Tor looked up. Galahad stood looking down on him, laughing — and there was Alin just getting to his feet, rubbing his eyes. He and Tor grinned at each other. Galahad looked out the door.

"Listen!" he said. "Here they come!"

Tor looked out. Down the path, knights and squires were marching with slow and stately tread. Sir Launcelot walked first, and at his shoulder hobbled old Father Ambrosius, priest of the chapel. Tor and Alin stood aside together in the shadowed doorway while the others entered, filling the little chapel, where they knelt behind Galahad for the prayers and blessings.

When these were over and all had passed quietly out, Alin and Tor stood just outside the doorway ready to follow. Three of the oldest squires — Hanay, Gorman, and Morvain — were carrying the pieces of Galahad's armor. Galahad himself had the lance and his sword. As he passed the two boys, he held out the lance to Tor and the sword to Alin.

So, last of all the group, Tor and Alin went up to the castle.

The first work of the new day was beginning. A bright fire flamed in the cookhouse; the clang of iron was ringing from Giles' anvil. Rimbot, coming from the mews with a bathing tub to empty, stood watching. Brok stood in the doorway, smiling as he saw Tor.

Into the oldest and largest tower went the procession. Alin walked slowly, holding the sword across his hands; beside him, Tor carried the lance straight in front of him.

As they went up the stone stairs, they heard the sounds of many voices. Looking through the doorway into the great hall, where the dim morning light was reinforced by many a torch, they saw one huge round table, taking up most of the space. At this table many knights were seated. Tor recognized most of those nearest — Sir Kay, Sir Ector, Sir Gareth, Sir Lamorack, the son of good King Pellinore of the Western Marshes.

King Arthur, the only one of them all in armor, sat among them, wearing his hauberk of the golden scales, with his sword, Excalibur, at his side. The

King's head was bare, and his hair fell waving down to his shoulders.

The boys stood looking. There was the empty seat at the table close to Arthur, with writing on the back of the chair — writing that seemed to move and to shine. Tor caught his breath, trembling. Touching Alin's arm, he felt it quiver too. This was the wondrous Round Table.

Following the rest, their eyes still on the Seat Perilous, they went into the hall, last of all those who crowded now to join the group. Behind them the churls from the bailey had begun to crowd and stare in with round and half-scared eyes, and then to make way, scrambling aside for Queen Guinevere and her damsels.

King Arthur held up his hand, and the knights stood. Then Sir Launcelot advanced to Arthur, knelt, and said:

"I crave the boon of knighthood from your Highness' grace for my son, Galahad."

The King made a sign, and Sir Launcelot arose and stood aside while Sir Gawaine spoke.

"If it be pleasing to the King, I will sponsor this youth."

Arthur looked around. Sir Tristram stepped forward.

"I too sponsor the lad."

The King beckoned to Galahad, and he went

forward and knelt before Arthur. Queen Guinevere signed to her damsels. Little Nimue went forward and, with Elaine's help, fastened on Galahad's heels his golden spurs. Then Enid and Lynette drew over his head the hauberk Brok had made for him, and Alin stepped forward with the sword.

King Arthur looked into Galahad's upraised face.

"Can you make, Galahad, the vow every knight must make — and repeat every year as long as he lives?"

Galahad's voice was strong and clear in answer:

"I make solemn promise to do no cruelty, but kindness; to grant mercy to him who asks it; to do no battle for the wrong, but to make wrongs right; to serve the weak; to show courtesy and service to gentlewomen and damsels — so long as life be in me or strength in my arms."

As still as statues were knights and ladies and the cluster of churls at the doorway. King Arthur stood and, taking Excalibur from his side, raised it and swung the blade flatwise upon Galahad's shoulder.

"Knight shall you be. Be brave, gentle, and true. Arise, Sir Galahad!"

A shout of welcome rose up from the knights:

"Hail, Sir Galahad!"

And to this the ladies added their chorus:

"Hail, Sir Galahad!"

There was shouting, too, among the churls

crowding at the door. Galahad stood, his face flushed and his clear eyes bright with happiness.

"There is but one seat empty." The King pointed. "It is for him who will one day be the greatest knight of all. But he who is unworthy of it dare not sit upon it. Will you take it, Sir Galahad?"

Sir Galahad, looking at the Seat Perilous, shook his head.

"Lord Arthur, it is not for me, the youngest and least of all this company to take that seat!"

There was a sound from the huddling churls as a tall blue-robed old man with a long white beard and a kinglike stateliness came slowly into the hall.

"Why! There is Father Kent! What is he doing here?" gasped Tor to Alin.

But the knights were saying joyfully:

"The Wizard Merlin has returned to Camelot!"

The old man greeted King Arthur and the Queen, and then held up his hand. All the sound of voices fell into silence.

"Let Sir Galahad take the Seat Perilous without fear," he commanded. "Look! The writing has stopped its motion and has written *Galahad*. It is to him that the Seat Perilous belongs, for he will do the greatest deed of all."

Sir Launcelot took Sir Galahad's hand and led him to the empty chair. As he took it, Queen Guinevere and her damsels passed from the hall.

Behind every knight stood his squire, but behind Sir Galahad stood no one.

"Whom will you choose for your squire, Sir Galahad?" asked King Arthur. "Here are many gallant and high-born pages old enough to become squires. Look around among them and choose."

Sir Galahad glanced around the wide and lofty hall. Torches flared above the great table, lighting the bright embroidered garments of the knights and the blue robes of Merlin. Young squires and pages, in green or red or yellow tunics, were grouped here and there. Looking over them all, Sir Galahad's eyes passed over many a boy who started forward, hand up. At last he seemed to find the one he was seeking. Alin was standing near Tor, his face full of eagerness, but making no movement. Finding him, Sir Galahad smiled and beckoned.

"I will choose Alin, if it please the King," he said. "He is strong and brave, and has proved himself true."

So Alin, leaving Tor, went swiftly and stood at Sir Galahad's shoulder to make his vow of loyalty. Then Galahad spoke to King Arthur again.

"Lord Arthur, I crave of you a boon."

"Speak, Sir Galahad," replied the King.

There was a quick silence in the high-arched hall.

Everyone wished to hear the boon asked by the newly made knight.

"There is one here who has deserved well of his King and all this company. For his kind deeds and his bravery and kindness, I beg that Tor of the village be made a page."

There was a movement of astonishment among the crowding, listening churls, for nothing like this had ever been heard of among them. King Arthur was looking curiously at Sir Galahad, and the eyes of every knight at the Round Table went as curiously from Tor to the King. Sir Launcelot seemed about to speak.

"Truly," the King said, "you shall have a page for your service, fair Sir Galahad, trained in all the duties of a page — in music, falconry, riding, and tilting, as well as in gentleness, obedience, and courtesy. But you know well that no churl is so trained, nor can be squire or knight. Ask another boon, for it grieves me to refuse you."

There was a deep-voiced murmur among the knights, and a shuffling of the callused feet of the watching churls. Tor, leaning on the lance, his face drawn with excitement, tried to hold himself straight and soldierly. His father's voice seemed to be murmuring in his ears:

"*Do not break your heart with such things. . . .*

Yet remember that a churl may be as noble as a king, if he wills . . ."

Merlin raised a gaunt old hand, and there was again silence that all might hear. Tor fastened his troubled eyes on the old hermit whom he had known as Father Kent. He felt, as always, that what the wise old man said was true and right. He listened eagerly as Merlin spoke.

"Lord Arthur, Tor needs no words of a king to make him worthy. He has that within himself which no king has put there and no king can take away. Many years have I known this lad, and my eyes seen much. There are those here present who could speak for him if it were needed: noble Sir Launcelot . . . young Alin . . . Rimbot . . . Brok . . . Sir Kay . . ."

As Merlin spoke their names, each started forward as if to speak, but the wizard went on calmly:

"All these could testify that young Tor is brave and unselfish, and altogether worthy of this boon. I too so testify."

King Arthur inclined his head.

"The wisdom of Merlin surpasses our own," he said. "Sir Galahad, you have our permission to take the lad Tor, son of Wain the cowherd, to train as a page."

Tor could hardly believe his ears. Galahad smiled

141

at his confusion, and Alin clapped his shoulder warmly. Among the waiting throng there rose such a clamor of rejoicing as roused even the white gerfalcon napping across the bailey in the mews.

It was mid-afternoon of the following day, a summer day as fair as any old Britain had ever known. Tor, who had been given a place among the pages in the castle, had gone down to the village in the morning to tell his family the wonderful news.

Leaving them as joyful as he was himself, he went back toward the castle, but stopped to wait by the ford. Here, he knew, he must say good-bye to Galahad and to Alin. On this day the new knight was to ride away into the world, to seek something which all knights had sought and would seek, but which, so said Merlin, was to be given to him alone. What this thing was Tor was not very sure, but he felt that if it were to be won by strength and goodness, Galahad would win it.

As the sun drew toward the west, Galahad and Alin rode down the hill. Galahad was mounted on a white charger, and Alin rode beside him on a hackney. Tor held up his hand and shouted, so they turned the horses toward him and stopped before crossing the ford.

Sir Galahad leaned down and held out his hand.

"Good-bye, Tor," he said. "Take care of Lila for me. Ride her when she is able again. And the colt — take him for your own. In a year and a day, watch for us here at the ford. Good-bye!"

Tor stood with pounding heart watching the two cross the stream. When, with a final waving of hands, they had disappeared into the overhanging woods, he turned and began running up the road toward the castle. Lila and the colt — *his* colt! — were waiting for him.